Romar Jones Takes a Hike

Advance Review Copy
Plicata Press LLC
PO Box 32, Gig Harbor WA 98335
www.plicatapress.com

Also By Jan Walker

A Farm in the South Pacific Sea (adult fiction)

An Inmate's Daughter (YA fiction)

Dancing to the Concertina's Tune: A Prison Teacher's Memoir

Parenting From A Distance (for incarcerated parents)

My Relationships, My Self

ROMAR JONES TAKES A HIKE

JAN WALKER

Plicata Press
Gig Harbor, Washington

Plicata Press LLC
P.O. Box 32

Gig Harbor, WA 98332
www.plicatapress.com

This is a work of fiction. Any similarity to real persons, living or dead, is coincidental and not intended by the author. Vesta's by the Sea is based on a resort no longer in existence.

ISBN: 978-0-9828205-9-9
LCCN: 2011917381

Walker, Jan
Romar Jones Takes a Hike / Jan Walker
1. Teen Adventure – Fiction   2. Roseburg, OR High School – Fiction
3. Oregon Coast – Fiction   4. Vesta's by the Sea – Fiction
5. Crystal Energy – Fiction   6. Relationships – Fiction
7. Washington Corrections Center for Women – Fiction
8. Teen Independent Living Program – Fiction

This is for all children of incarcerated parents ...
"It's not your fault."

1

TAKE A HIKE

Roseburg High School, Roseburg Oregon

Mr. Whitley roamed the classroom, eyes taking in students and the work on their desks. Romar Jones hunkered low, head bent over his unfinished elements of poetry assignment, Rec Specs dangling like an amulet against myopia. He used that thought for symbol, then struggled with alliteration until *Sunny summer Sunday* popped into his head.

Worked great, except it was Friday, the first of June, freshman English. School would be out in a couple weeks. Uncle Sherman and Aunt Joan would ship him out of Roseburg on a Greyhound bus.

They'd dropped that piece of news the night before when they got upset over the sound of his basketball on the driveway. He'd had a good dribble pattern going when his uncle yelled, "Knock it off. We're trying to catch a breeze, not the tap-tap-tap of a bouncing ball."

Romar went inside, said, "Sorry," and headed for his room.

His uncle stopped him on the third step. "Now that your grandmother's dead there's no need to keep you here with us. Arlene and her husband can use your help in their orchard."

Their orchard would be acres of dust, he knew that much from listening to Aunt Arlene the two times they'd met.

Dust motes drifted over his classroom desk. He caught one in a circle made by his thumb and forefinger, and got a simile out of it, the mote like a basketball dropping through a hoop.

At his granny's funeral the preacher said, "We come from dust, we return to dust." He guessed that might be a metaphor. Granny died in

March. His uncle and aunt did their Jones' family duty by letting him stay with them until the school year ended. In two weeks they'd ship him down to Medford to work in dusty fields.

Granny had planned to take him west to the Oregon coast, to the town where she grew up, for summer break. One of these days, he'd take her ashes, a kind of dust, to the coast. Not all her ashes, just the handful he swiped from the urn before Uncle Sherman delivered it to Roseburg Cemetery.

He was still finishing up the first assignment when Mr. Whitley handed out the next one. Write a poem using at least one of the elements. Make it something that relates to life. Basketball and Granny were the elements of life that kept Romar going after his dad was killed. He and Granny stayed on a few months in the Glide house that had always been home. Long enough to finish seventh grade. He'd liked his life there. He, his dad and Granny were a happy family.

Then Uncle Sherman, his dad's older brother, came along and took over as the reigning male relative, the one who could make decisions.

During the two years Romar lived in Roseburg, one year in junior high, one in high school, he'd played center on the schools' basketball teams. He'd write a poem related to basketball. No way would he write about Dad or Granny or death, either by accident or by getting old.

"Two minutes," Whitley said, roaming the room, down one aisle and up the other.

Romar grabbed his pencil and scribbled the thought that came to mind at that moment. In what seemed like less than two minutes, Whitley called on him.

"Jones, sit up straight and read what you've got."

He struggled into an upright position and pulled his glasses into place. Whitley stopped beside his desk.

"Lose the glasses. No sports gear in this classroom. You know the rules. Short as that work is, you should be able to recite it without looking at your paper."

Romar let the specs fall back on his chest and recited the thought he'd submit as his poem, spoken the way he heard it.

Poetry . . . makes no sense . . .
Makes me feel. . . like I'm dense.

The chords in Whitley's neck bulged, a sign that he'd lost his patience. "Poetry is not rap." He grabbed the paper, wrinkled it and tossed it toward the waste basket.

"Air ball," Romar said, sotto voce. He'd learned that term in class. Whitley called on a girl who cried while reading about her dog dying. Romar slid back down in his seat, lowered his head and put his emotions in check. No way would he let anyone see his sadness. The girl got high praise. Two wadded papers landed beside his. Three more poems, all written by girls, earned Whitley's approval. The guy across the aisle, one of his basketball teammates, wrinkled his paper and tossed it without bothering to read.

"Okay, listen up," Whitley said. "Your next assignment is to analyze one of William Stafford's works. *Security.*" Whitley studied under Stafford. That made the poet a big deal.

Romar squinted at the photocopied words. Something grabbed him. He read the poem a second time, concentrating on the meaning, blocking out voices reading lines aloud. Maybe poetry did make sense. Living with Uncle Sherman and Aunt Joan provided him with security, but security wasn't enough without Granny there.

"Jones," Whitley bellowed.

That brought him straight up. "Yeah?"

"Where are you?"

"Uh, right at the end. '... *turn to the open sea and let go.*'"

Whitley rolled his eyes. "I meant metaphorically. Sit up straight and pay attention, or take a hike."

Take a hike, as in report to the principal's office, rat yourself out, prepare for prison time in after school detention. He'd taken a hike once before, he knew the drill. At that moment it sounded like a good plan. Paying attention had been hard ever since Granny died. She'd pop into his thoughts at odd times – thoughts that made his eyes get wet.

As for prison, he knew a bit about that, too. Not as much as he'd need to know to find his mother, if he decided to go looking for her. Granny wanted to help him, but she died before Romar got any solid information. Not much to go on, just prison and Washington state. Aunt Joan gave up that much during one of her rants about being stuck with an overgrown teenage guy just when she'd gotten her two girls off to college.

Okay, all the thinking did it. Wet eyes, regardless of rapid blinking. He put the Rec Specs on for cover, shoved the photocopy of Stafford's poem into his notebook and everything on his desk into his book bag. Some clown in the front row stuck out his feet. Romar gave them a kick and stumbled to the door.

The long hallway floor looked like a narrow basketball court. He practiced his dribble dance, skinny hips shifting. He feinted left, then drove the key – the open-door-policy office positioned just inside the school's entrance. The woman on duty held a phone to her ear with her left shoulder and stabbed a piece of paper with a pen that wouldn't work. The paper slid to the floor. She glanced at him and shook her head. Whitley's hikers annoyed her. He backed away, eyes on her like she was the shot clock. She retrieved the paper, got the ink flowing. He counted down the seconds.

"Bzzzt, time's up."

She ignored him. Maybe it didn't sound clever to her. He walked away, expecting her to call him back. When she didn't, he pushed open the school's double doors, stepped outside and gulped in air coming off the Umpqua River.

Cars zipped past the school on the interstate that stretched from Mexico to Canada. He could hitch north to Washington, start looking for his mother. Or he could head west with Granny's ashes. Make the trip they'd planned. That's what he heard Granny saying in his head.

"Take me home, Romie. Home to Smelt Sands Beach."

That happened a lot – Granny talking to him. His counselor called it grief work; his few friends who knew called it weird. Maybe Whitley would say it was the creative muse at work. Nah, more likely he'd say, "Bull."

Romar looked around, still expecting to be ordered back inside. No kids heading across the lot from the mini-mart next to the school campus. No one, far as he could see. He jogged around parked cars, down under the interstate, across the Umpqua at the golf course. Nice day for golf; nice day for a hike.

His uncle and aunt's huge house felt eerie without any sign of Granny. They got rid of her things right after she died, erasing her presence like they'd erased his dad's after the accident. Sold everything except his dad's backpack and the gear it held. Romar had that in his closet.

Granny had said, "All Roland's things rightfully belong to Romar," but it hadn't mattered to Aunt Joan. She said, "There are debts to be paid. Funeral expenses, that rig that hauled the wrecked truck up out of the canyon."

It took Romar ten minutes, maybe less, to cram clothes that still fit him into stuff bags and fit the money pouch Granny made over his dad's belt. The pouch held one hundred fifty-four dollars. The belt needed another hole punched to fit, so he shoved it in the pack, too, and grabbed his ugly black frame glasses held together with electrical tape, black on black. Best he could do until he had more money.

In the kitchen, he cadged a loaf of bread, sliced ham, cheese and a nearly empty bottle of mustard from Aunt Joan's refrigerator, and wrapped them with the ice packs he kept for icing his ankles after a game. He added two cans of tuna, ten hot cocoa mix packets and four energy bars. They'd make it easier to stomach the old dehydrated pouches of food stored in his dad's bear-resistant container. One bite of pack food, one bite of bar, like a reward for eating his vegetables.

He poured a glass of milk, studied the official Oregon State map his aunt kept in a drawer, and plotted a route that kept him on back roads. He downed a second glass of milk while he wrote a note to his uncle and aunt and taped it to the milk carton. Since it was Friday, they'd stay in town for dinner and dart games. Chances were good they wouldn't find the note until the next day.

I'm going to Washington to find my mother. I know she's in prison. There are some things I need to ask her. Like you said when Granny and I moved in here, I'm big enough to be making my own way in the world.

Romar Andrew Jones.

He didn't mention Medford, or that he'd been thinking about taking off the last day of school, one day before they planned to put him on the bus.

He filled the backpack's water bottles and dropped them into their insulated holders. The pack smelled like his dad. He adjusted it, loosened his Rec Specs headband and walked out the door, his dad and Granny leaving with him in his thoughts.

By his best estimate he'd made it five miles before he needed food. An energy bar at least. He leaned his pack against a street-sign and mopped sweat from his face with his tee shirt. The street sign said Turkey Crick Lane. He was thinking that Whitley'd go ballistic at the word Crick when a wild turkey landed a few feet away and squawked at him.

"Okay, okay," he said, breaking off a piece of bar.

The turkey cocked its head and took off without grabbing the bite. She disappeared in a grassy field across the road. A second later Romar heard the sound of a vehicle. A shiny red pickup rounded the corner. He grabbed his pack, thinking red truck, Uncle Sherman. No way even his skinny body could hide behind a signpost.

2

RIVER CAMPS

The truck braked, skidded on gravel and backed up. A 4-door, gun rack on the back window just like Uncle Sherman's, but a Ford. His uncle drove a GMC. Romar took a breath.

The passenger window lowered. A guy's voice said, "Dude! What's up?"

Romar lowered his head and put a name with the face. Josh Mobley, Roseburg High varsity basketball center and team captain.

"Mobley?" Romar said, taking in the truck's interior. Leather seats, music in surround sound, lighted buttons and levers to rival an airplane console. Not that he'd ever been inside an airplane, but he'd seen pictures.

"Yeah. Where you headed, man, loaded down like that?"

"A campground on the river."

"Hey, sounds great. Want a ride? I can take you far as the intersection."

"Yeah, great," Romar said, figuring 'great' worked since Josh used it first. He didn't know what intersection Josh meant, but a ride got him more distance from Roseburg.

"Toss your pack in back, make sure there's nothing sharp poking out of your pockets, don't want to scar the seats," Josh said.

Romar let the pack slide off his shoulders and lifted it into the truck bed. He ran his hands over his pants to be sure nothing poked through a pocket, and settled in the dark gray leather.

"You live out there?" he asked Josh.

"Nah, not hardly. I work at the winery. The Henry Estate, I hoe weeds and shit like that."

Romar's head jerked. He'd been staring straight ahead, envious of Josh, still startled by the red truck.

"Yeah? That's what I'm supposed to do this summer. Hoe weeds, I mean, but in Medford."

"Medford. What's Medford got that you can't find in Roseburg?"

"Some relatives with a pear orchard. They're looking for cheap labor."

"Gottcha," Josh said. "I just got hired at the winery in April, after basketball season ended, because my old man knows the manager. Only problem, my car's not running right now so I have to hit up my folks to use their wheels or else hitch."

"This your dad's truck?"

Josh nodded and flashed a smile Romar's way. "You've got it. He'll be pacing the floor until he sees it back in the driveway tonight. He'll walk around it, inspect every inch, even the tires."

Romar groaned like he knew how dads were about sons driving their vehicles. "You're going to the university in the fall, right?"

"Yep, I'll be a University of Oregon Duck. Or a duckling, more 'n likely. Bench warmer."

"No way, man, you'll be a starter on the freshman squad."

"You think?" Josh said. "Hell, I'm only six feet tall, you're taller 'n me already. Coach Kramer had his eyes on you all season, boo-hooing that he couldn't raid the frosh team. You'll be varsity center next year."

"I doubt that," Romar said. "There's guys ahead of me." Chances were, he'd be working a minimum wage job somewhere in Washington, lying about his age, shooting hoops in garbage cans in an alley.

"Catch you next week," Josh said when they reached the intersection.

"Yeah. Thanks for the ride." Romar finished the power bar he'd started at Turkey Crick Lane, drank half a bottle of water and headed northwest. His feet and empty stomach both ached by the time he found the campground he'd noted on his aunt's map.

He set up his dad's tent in a wash under willow branches, out of sight from the highway. A flat rock served as a table for sandwich making. After two ham and cheese sandwiches, he soaked his feet in the icy river. Before darkness fell, he zipped himself inside the tent for his first night as a man alone in the world. Six feet-two, skinny, whiskers on his face, dark hair grown longish since Granny died. No Uncle Sherman there to remind him he was big enough to make his own way in the world.

The next morning Romar set out, determined to make Elkton, on the bend of the Umpqua, before dark. A man could hike thirty miles on paved road.

He stopped at a public campground on the river, only halfway to his destination. His shoulders ached, his feet burned, his stomach begged for food. Worst of all, his nerves jumped around like a downed electric wire, shooting worry sparks into his brain. It seemed like a hundred red pickups passed him, all of them slowing down to take a look. He tried to disguise himself by pulling a tee shirt over his head so it covered his hair and hung down over his pack.

He dropped his pack, sat beside it, knees to chest. Before he could ease his swollen feet out of his shoes, two boys ran past him, shouting and cussing like loggers wrestling a hang-up. They looked alike, both too young to know such cuss words, so Granny said in his head.

He opened his pack and dug around for Second Skin for blisters, his eyes on the boys. Both went down, face first, on slippery rocks. Served them right. The smaller one didn't come up. Romar pushed himself back onto his feet, looking around for adults. No one in sight. He went in the river after them, shoes still on. The cold water felt good, for a few seconds.

He slipped his arms around the smaller boy and lifted. The boy squirmed and spit at his brother. "He's acting, he's not hurt," the bigger boy said. "Get up on your own two feet and take it back."

"Pig brain, pig brain, pig brain," the squirming armful said.

Romar struggled to keep him upright. Blood gushed from under blond hair on the boy's forehead, ran onto his right eyebrow and dripped down the side of his face. Romar saw the lump forming and wondered if the kid might have a concussion.

"He's hurt. Get your parents. Get help."

The bigger kid hesitated.

"Go," Romar said. He settled the injured boy on his bottom above the river's edge and tried to remember if he should lay him on his back or stomach, or keep him sitting upright. He cupped water in one hand, washed the wound and looked around for leaves for a compress. None in sight and a screaming kid with blood running down his face.

"Hold on," Romar said. He pulled off his shirt, dipped it in the river and pressed it to the gash. Great. Now he had wet shoes, a bloody shirt and a sobbing kid with a runny nose.

A woman's voice called, "Preston? Are you all right?"

The kid sputtered, "My mom," and cried louder.

The woman removed the soggy tee, inspected the wound, said "Oh, God."

Romar said, "I'll get a real compress."

The woman yelled, "Hunter, you get your butt down here this minute."

That drew Romar's eyes to the woman's butt, a nice one for a mother. Her shorts stretched when she bent over the boy. Her legs were nice, too.

The woman yelled "Hunter," again when the bigger boy showed up with a man whose grip on his arm must have cut off circulation to his brain.

"He's a dumb shit," Hunter said.

"Hunter, watch your mouth."

"I can't watch my mouth, it's below my eyes, it's impossible."

"You're impossible," the mother said.

The wounded boy sniffed a couple times, said "Pig brain, pig brain," and leaned against his mother's legs.

The man extended a hand to Romar. "Austin Matlock, call me Mat. My wife Julie, our sons Preston and Hunter."

"Mat, for God's sake get a bandage, Pres is bleeding here."

Mr. Matlock took gauze and tape from Romar and handed it to his wife. "She's better at cuts and scrapes."

"There's a lump, not just the gash," Romar said. "You're supposed to watch for concussion."

"We'll watch," Mrs. Matlock said. "Mat, carry Pres back to the camper. Hunter, you and I will have a discussion." She handed Romar his wet tee shirt.

Romar watched them go, a family camping along the river. He wondered how his mother would have handled a bleeding head wound. His dad would have cleaned it with something sterile, made a butterfly bandage, asked stupid questions and watched eyes for enlarged pupils. His dad had been a river and wilderness guide on the North Umpqua River and in the national forest. He'd taught Romar how to care for wounds.

The river went from silver white where the late afternoon sun glistened to charcoal where trees cast shadows. Romar listened to the water moving over rocks and wondered how one of Whitley's poets would describe it. Words wouldn't work. You had to hear the sound. In his head he was back on the North Umpqua, the main river's tributary that he'd lived beside from birth to a few months after his dad's death. His dad's truck had gone down a steep bank along the river. The guys who got him out and called for an ambulance said they'd found a deer hung up in the wreckage. Big buck, they said. Nice rack. Romar still wondered if they'd kept the antlers.

He gathered wood, got a fire going, got his shoes staked by it to dry. An hour or so later he heard a voice, Mr. Matlock, saying "Hey, man, you roasting shoes for dinner?"

Romar laughed, figuring the man meant to be funny. "Nah, dinner'll be beef stroganoff." His dad said that always impressed hikers and fishermen who'd be hungry enough to like whatever reconstituted food they got. He couldn't get his dad out of his thoughts.

"Backpacker's fare, am I right?" Mr. Matlock asked. "How about saving that for another day and joining us for hamburgers? Julie says there's more than enough. She wants to thank you for seeing to our boys."

"That's okay. I don't need any more thanks."

"It's not okay with my wife. She said no dinner for me if I come back without you. Said to bring your wet shoes along, she'll stick 'em in the oven."

"Oven?"

"Yeah, motor home oven. Makes camping a whole lot easier when you've got a wife, a couple kids." Matlock looked at Romar's tent. "You young guys, you can take off on foot, stop wherever you like, pee in the woods, that's freedom."

"Yeah, and I'm too grubby for a motor home."

"Don't worry about that. We barbecue outside. Slip on some sandals and come along with me."

"Uh, I didn't pack any sandals. Just the cross-trainers and some hiking boots that seem to have shrunk since last time I was out." They were his dad's boots, a bit too small, but he'd brought them anyway. He'd keep them forever, a reminder of his dad. Maybe he'd write a poem about them. Scuffed leather, broken laces.

"Well, hell, man, we'll take care of that. You've got big feet like me. There's extras in a storage compartment in my rig. I'll have Preston run 'em down."

Romar had two thick burgers with tomato and onion slices, two root beers, more potato chips than Granny would ever allow and four Oreo cookies. The Teva sandals worked. Mr. Matlock said to keep them, they were a couple years old, the sole tread a little worn.

"Hey, I remember what it's like, school sucking up all your spare change, getting by best you can. Where you headed?"

Mr. Matlock got it in his head that Romar was on break from college. When the conversation got to destination, he said the coast, without being specific.

"Us, too," Matlock said. "Winchester Bay. Deep sea fishing for me, campground time for Julie and the boys."

"I'm heading north from Reedsport," Romar said, glad he'd studied the map closely enough to know that Winchester Bay was south of the junction with the coast highway.

"Toward Florence?" Mrs. Matlock asked. "I want to go up there after Mat's through fishing."

"Might as well travel in style far as Reedsport," Matlock said before Romar could answer. "Ride along with us, give your feet and back a rest, help Julie keep the boys entertained. They're on early release slash summer vacation. She's helping them finish some school work."

Romar protested, sounding like Granny, but the Matlocks wouldn't listen. He thought about the advantages. Getting to Reedsport the next day would be like getting a free throw for a technical foul. Still, he'd have to be on guard every minute, think before opening his mouth. Slip up once, say the wrong thing and momentum could shift. They could deliver him to a police station.

3

THE COAST

The Matlocks' motor home had leather seats up front, hardwood floors, nice kitchen, nice furniture. "State of the art," Matlock said. He spread a towel on a bed and laid Romar's pack on it. The boys had a movie in a DVD player and a bag of popcorn.

Mrs. Matlock said, "Call me Julie." She read aloud from travel and winery brochures. "Brandborg will be our first stop. The winery. Elkton has two wineries. I want a case of their 2004 Pinot Gris."

She showed the winery brochure to Romar, who would never have gotten *pee no gree* out of that spelling. He wondered if his mother liked wine? Or just illegal drugs? He'd overheard Aunt Joan say his mother had gotten into meth.

They stopped at a second winery. Mr. Matlock loaded two more cases into the motor home. A little after noon they pulled into a restaurant on the river for lunch. Romar offered Mr. Matlock money, to no avail. Lucky for him, but worrisome. He didn't like to owe anyone for anything. Two years with his uncle and aunt had taught him that.

The Matlocks dropped him off on a side street in Reedsport, two blocks before the Coast Highway. Mr. Matlock handed him a business card along with his pack. "I wanted to give you a couple bottles of wine for the hike, but Julie's sure you're not twenty-one. She worries about legalities."

"I just want to give you a hug," Julie Matlock said. "You remind me of my youngest brother. And I worry about kids getting caught up in alcohol for other than legal reasons. Call Mat's cell phone when you're settled. Maybe we can catch up with you in Florence."

Romar thought Mr. Matlock should have worried about that hug. Other than Granny, who hugged him every day including the day she died, he'd only been that close to one other woman, Aunt Arlene. He barely knew her. The hug was one of those grab and squeeze things at Granny's funeral. Arlene and her alcoholic husband were the relatives in Medford who needed cheap summer help.

"Here, take this, I'll pick up another one when we stop at the lighthouse." Mrs. Matlock poked a booklet into his hand. Oregon Coast Mile-By-Mile Guide to Highway 101. "And call us on the cell. Anytime. We want to keep in touch with you. Who knows what would have happened with our boys if you weren't there."

"Keep us in the loop," Mr. Matlock said when he shook Romar's hand.

When the motor home disappeared from sight, he looked at the business card. Matlock Enterprises, Sacramento, California. It didn't say what enterprises, but Romar figured they provided a lot of money. Maybe he'd look for a job in Florence, stay there long enough to get a new frame for his glasses. Long enough for Julie Matlock to find him. He wouldn't mind getting another hug from her.

He hoisted his pack and set out. It felt good to be walking again, moving his legs. He stopped in the middle of the bridge that crossed the Umpqua River. "Julie," he said to the wind.

The town of Gardiner, two miles north of Reedsport, had a small store. He bought a handful of energy bars. They came to almost ten dollars.

The clerk, an older woman, asked, "Where you headed?"

Oh oh, pop quiz. "Uh, over to the beach, soon as I find the road."

"Sparrow Park Road?" Before he could nod, or admit he didn't know the area, she said, "That's a couple miles, then four or so across the dunes before you reach the Pacific."

"Yeah," he said, thinking he should have looked at Julie's highway guide.

"Watch where you set up camp out there. Some of those dune buggy drivers get a little crazy."

"Yeah, thanks." He pictured headlines in the local newspaper: *Runaway teen run over by dune buggy.*

An old, partly demolished lumber mill along the highway looked as lonely as he felt. He leaned into a climb as 101 went uphill, stopped at the sign marked Sparrow Park Road, opened the guide. "Julie," he said again. She'd been nice to him. A few more hours with her and he'd have told her everything.

A red pickup sped by. His heart sped up. Sweat erupted. He waited for it to brake to a stop. He heaved a sigh when it kept going. Still, being found, having someone to talk to, might not be so bad.

On Monday morning, seventy-two hours after walking out of Whitley's class, Romar got his first glimpse of the Pacific Ocean from an overlook along the highway. Mountains of sand made up the shifting dunes. The coast highway guide called the view spectacular. Whitley would blow the foul whistle. Spectacular didn't tell the reader a darn thing. He started a poem for Whitley's class, something to send in someday so he could get a decent grade.

Sun glistened on waves
Waves washed sand
Sand stung a bearded face.

So much for poetry. Forget the grade. He had something more important than school and grades to think about. His mother. He didn't even know what she looked like. As for the poem, overcast skies made the sun part a lie.

He figured he could make Florence from the overlook by three or four in the afternoon, if he hiked the highway. Instead, he stumbled down the steep slope toward the waves. He added another line to his poem: *Sand in shoes, biting.* Whitley might like the biting part.

He leaned his pack against a drift log, emptied his shoes, shook his socks and rolled up his pant legs. Fine grains stuck to leg hair. He stamped his foot; they held on. *Static cling.* He'd add that as the fifth line.

Warm, loose sand transitioned to a cool, packed surface. Whitley was big on transitions. Waves washed around his ankles. Sand slithered out from under his feet. He chased the outgoing water and dashed away from the incoming until a breaker caught him, soaking his pant legs up to his butt. Time to move on.

When water and an energy bar no longer satisfied his hunger, he stopped to heat the remainder of the reconstituted potatoes he'd cooked in camp the night before. He used the inland side of a drift log as a backrest and shelter for his stove, and stretched out his legs. He was scraping up the last bite of potatoes when he heard a voice.

"Yo, buddy."

An unshaved man with oily hair rose out of the dunes like a cartoon monster rising from the sea. The man was two or three inches shorter than Romar. His overcoat swept the ground. Sleeves fell to his fingers.

"Got a drink there for a parched soul?" Drool leaked from his mouth onto his matted beard.

"Uh, not really."

The man moved closer. He stank, like he peed in his clothes.

"Just a nip for an old man. Need to warm my insides. I won't drain you dry."

"Like whisky, you mean?" Romar was on his feet, judging distances between himself and the man, whose breath reeked. Meth mouth, he'd bet. Could be that's what smelled like pee. He'd found pictures online on the library computer after Aunt Joan said his mother had gotten into meth. Gross pictures of face sores and rotting teeth. Plus information about the odor associated with making the stuff. And now a gross smell.

"Whisky, gin, vodka, whatever you've got. I'm not picky, man."

"All I've got's water, and I've been drinking from it."

The beard and moustache moved, exposing rotting teeth. "Water'll rust your pipes. C'mon, dig into that pack and pull out your bottle for your old buddy here. Hell, I served our country in combat, least you can do is serve me a small drink."

Romar stuffed his stove, dirty utensils and garbage into his pack without taking his eyes off his opponent. "I don't carry alcohol, I'm underage, for one thing and I don't like what drinking and drugs make people do." He stepped over the log that had shielded his stove, ready to run, ready to knock the guy to the ground if it took that to get out of his reach.

"A smoke, then. I'll settle for a smoke."

"Forget it. I'm an athlete. No smoking, no using. Find someone else. There's campgrounds all along here." Romar backed away, watching eyes above the shaggy beard, the shoulder position that could telegraph which way the guy would move. Something changed; the man's shoulders drooped, his eyes shifted. Time to take the shot.

Romar turned and jogged away, his pack's hip straps unbuckled. He kept up the pace longer than necessary, enjoying the workout but thinking about the man. The bad teeth signaled meth mouth. From what he'd read, the guy could get crazy with need for a fix.

When he reached a wide swath of water crossing the beach, he turned inland and found a campground. He cleaned his cook gear, refilled his water bottles and dug his dad's skinning knife out of his pack. Should have had it hooked it on his jeans all along.

Back on the beach, the dunes got wider and higher, some bare sand, some grassy, some covered with evergreen trees. He headed east to the highway where he could make better time. He climbed, descended and walked along what served as a path at the base of intersecting dunes. His footfalls started a dune avalanche that filled his shoes. He dumped sand, chugged a bottle of water, ate an energy bar. With his pack settled and his knife at the ready, he set out, following tracks left by other hikers.

No sound reached him, no crashing waves or rustling tree branches. It occurred to him that the tracks had led him in a circle. He climbed to the top of a dune and saw taller dunes all around, a grassy flat below and no sun to direct him. Had he come by the evergreen trees partially buried in sand to his left? Or those slightly behind and off to his right? His heart pounded like he'd raced the length of the basketball court with an entire team a half-step behind.

Lost in the wilderness. His dad would be disappointed in him, his granny worried. "Damn," he said, with a silent apology to Granny for muttering even that mild expletive. "Jones fouls out."

4

QUAGMIRES

That way? No, that way.

Granny and his dad talking in his head. It would help if the overcast lifted, let him see the sun, which would be well into the west. He headed for the grassy flat, figuring it would be easier than slogging through deep sand. His feet sank into muck that tugged at his knees. He shortened and lightened his stride, reached level ground, and let out his breath. Another dune rose across the meadow. He'd head for it. One step, a sucking sound, a second step, made to correct his balance. Quicksand? He went on tilt, face forward. He windmilled his arms to straighten up. Ass first would beat face first.

"Dad?" he said. As prayers go, it wasn't much. But it said everything about being a man on his own in the world. He looked over his shoulder. One long step back would save him if he could get a foot out. Did he figure that out on his own, or was his dad answering?

He unhooked his dad's trenching tool, wrested off the pack and half pushed, half flung it behind him. Thunk. Solid ground. He worked his right foot, twisting and lifting until it came free, shoe stuck on his toe and filled with muck at the heel. He pulled it off, threw it over his shoulder and took a giant step back. His left leg seemed bent backward at the ankle. It felt like it might snap off. That would be the end of playing basketball, even in alleys. He wiggled, feeling like he'd entered a contortionist contest. Finally, the sand's grip on his foot loosened enough for his aching ankle to do the twist. He twisted and tugged, getting his hips into the action. His foot came out with a slurp, like a kid sucking the last of a milkshake through a fat straw. No shoe. His glasses slipped down his sweaty nose. The swamp would eat them in one gulp. How many times had he tried to lose them so replacements would be required?

He shoved the broken glasses in his jeans pocket, lifted his dangling Rec Specs into place and snapped his dad's trenching tool into working mode. Dig, slurp. Dig, sluuurrrp, sluuurrp. Hole filling fast, arm in muck to elbow, to biceps, to armpit. Fingers on shoe. Pull, tug, twist. Tug, twist, pull. He felt his shoulders strain like he'd set the weight machine too high. The sand was letting go, the shoe moving. Tugging, sucking sound, one arm churning air, falling backward, shovel and shoe and muck on top of him.

Lost. Sand and muck on his legs and arms and clothes. Shoes heavy as lead weights. Clouds thickening overhead. Granny and his dad came into his head at the same moment.

Study the dunes' shapes, ripples on the sand, the way trees have been bent by the wind. Watch the cloud movement. Wind blows inland from the ocean most of the time.

He watched, turned ninety degrees to what should be north, took baby steps along the edge of the grassy bog. His feet were bare; grit chafed his legs. The marsh dried and ended with a stretch of smallish dunes. He faced what he'd determined to be east and focused like he would on making a shot. He studied the divots his feet made, then footprints he found, certain he'd come upon a path that led around another marsh and up a gradual slope.

Voices, or maybe trees talking to the wind, broke the silence. He crested the dune and looked down on blue water, a small boat, someone swimming. He leaped and shot an imaginary basketball. Slam dunk. He'd stumbled into the large state park with lakes and campsites, a place he thought he'd passed an hour ago.

He wanted to fling off his pack and run with arms spread wide, right into the lake. But the day's ordeals warned him to take guard. Danger lurked. He'd stepped right into a natural quagmire. Earlier, he'd jogged away from a human one. The human's eyes haunted him. Bloodshot eyes. Werewolf need? He imagined fangs behind the shaggy beard and moustache. The guy's bad breath could have come from something worse than meth. Could be he hacked lone hikers into small pieces, roasted them over a campfire and washed them down with blood.

Hikers fell off cliffs, boaters capsized, kids disappeared, never to be found. He read enough news, watched enough TV to hear those stories. His mother was a story, so said Aunt Joan. A meth head caught cooking and selling. She'd done time in Oregon, gotten out, gone to Washington, gotten arrested again. He learned all sorts of things when Aunt Joan went into a rant. Maybe the guy back down the beach had been one of his mother's partners. He should have asked, "Yo, buddy, you know Marlene Jones?"

His mother had named him for his dad and herself. Roland and Marlene. He sat on the sand and laughed until tears ran down his face. It sounded like crying. Sobbing, actually. Romar Jones, named for a dead dad and an incarcerated mother.

When he'd regained his composure, he followed a trail that circled to his right around the south end of the lake. Kids in shorts and tee shirts or bathing suits slid down the dunes on snow platters to the lake's edge. Young kids, younger than him. School buses with drivers standing around glancing at their watches waited in the parking lot.

He followed signs to a campground loop, found a water faucet without anyone around, rinsed his shoes and used his dad's knife to dig muck out of the soles. They could stand some scrubbing, maybe some bleach. The tread should get him to Washington, to his mother's current prison.

Three girls came around a bend and stopped to watch. Two had long blonde hair they knew how to swish with a shake of their heads. One had short black hair and big black eyes. They must have been sixth or seventh graders, not developed like high school girls but not flat chested like ten year olds. Romar sheathed the knife. Some adult might come along and go ballistic like adults tended to do when a tall sweaty guy and cute girls stood on the same patch of earth.

"Whatcha doin'," the girl with dark hair asked.

"Cleaning quicksand muck out of my shoes."

The shorter blonde said, "Are you, like, hiking?"

The tall blonde said, "Like duh, Mandy. Look at his pack, that's not exactly for carrying school books."

"Can we see what's inside?" the one called Mandy asked, one hand on a side-pocket zipper.

"Knock it off," the taller blonde said. "Didn't you see his knife? He could be like a killer or a rapist."

Mandy gasped and did something with her hands over her chest. Her head swayed so the blonde hair swirled left and right and left again.

"You girls better get back to your bus," he said. "The drivers had the engines revved up, ready to go."

The taller blonde and the girl with dark hair each grabbed one of Mandy's arms and pulled her along the loop road, giggling as they went. Romar watched them and wondered if they'd tell the bus drivers or some other supervisor that they'd encountered a man with a knife in the campground. Would they say man or boy? Most likely they'd say guy. "Some guy's in there with a knife." He hadn't shaved that morning. His beard wasn't what could be called heavy, but it could be called hairy. "Some guy with a hairy face is in there with a knife."

Reality check: he was a runaway teen with a few dollars, some good hiking gear, a container of his granny's ashes in his pack and his dad's knife in his pocket. He needed to get out to the highway before those bus drivers came looking for him or reported him to park authorities. He didn't have a park pass; he didn't belong there.

He could be arrested for brandishing a knife. Brandishing. Great word. He'd fit it into a poem.

He'd gotten less than a mile north of the park entrance when the buses passed him. Girls shouted from open windows. A few rain sprinkles fell. Rain, another problem for a hiker, an aggravation, like those girls.

He ate an energy bar, wishing it were an apple or orange or grapes, and marched on, those girls with him like they were on a screen on his Rec Specs. The rain got heavier, chilling his bare feet in Mr. Matlock's old Tevas. Black hair on his big toes curled. Did girls' toes grow hair that they shaved like their legs and under their arms?

He'd need clean socks for job hunting in Florence. Clean socks and Tevas. No motor home oven to dry his shoes; no campground fire unless he paid for a site in a state park. Find a job, hang out around RV parks, watch for Julie. For all the Matlocks. That was his plan.

Almost every shop on Bay Street in Old Town Florence had Help Wanted signs: tee shirts, art gallery, kite shop, women's clothes, none of them options for him. He went into a restaurant that looked big enough to need a busboy, peeled off his poncho in the entry, shook it and went through two sets of double doors. He'd never asked a business for a job. It wasn't exactly like offering to mow lawns or cut and stack wood.

A woman with her hair pulled back from her pock-marked face, dressed in white shirt and black skirt, said "It's early for lunch. We don't serve until eleven."

"Uh, no, uh, I'm looking for a job. Like, busing dishes?" His poncho dripped on the floor. He couldn't believe he'd said like and that he'd made it a question.

The woman looked at the poncho and then at him. "I'll get the manager."

A tall man dressed in black slacks and white dress shirt, unbuttoned but ironed, came back with the woman. "We're not hiring," he said, "but you can leave an application." Before Romar could mutter another 'uh', the man said, "What's with the backpack? You homeless?"

"Uh, no, it's summer break, I just got out here. To the coast, I'm looking for a job and a place to stay."

"Better find the place first, son. That pack's off-putting, if you know what I mean."

"Well, thanks." Romar went through the first set of double doors. *Off-putting?*

The next place didn't serve until eleven either. He carried his pack with the poncho folded and tucked under a strap so he could set the whole thing on the floor. A female voice from the kitchen area called out, "We're not open."

"Are you hiring for busing? Or dishwashing?"

"No, sorry," the voice said. "Try the fast food places out on the highway. Most restaurants down here have summer help lined up. Locals home from college." The owner of the voice appeared, an older woman with gray curly hair. She looked at him and the pack leaning against his leg. "You're not the guy that walked away from prison camp a couple weeks back? Nah, you're too young. Height and hair color about right, though." She had a nice smile, probably a nice mother to somebody.

"Thanks anyway," he said, hefting his pack and heading for the door. So, a guy walked away from prison. Could be he'd met the guy in the dunes. It would fit.

"Or you might check the docks. Some of the fishermen or crabbers might need a hand."

"Yeah, okay," Romar said. No way would he get a job gutting fish. If Julie Matlock ever did find him, he wanted to be clean enough for a hug. He walked back the way he'd come, socks soaked by the time he reached the highway. More than soaked twenty blocks later when he smelled fries coming from McDonalds. One order wouldn't break him. He stood in line, asked for the manager instead of fries. A young guy came out, nodded his head toward a booth. Romar put his pack on the bench and sat beside it.

"Name's Jeff," the guy said. "Got your food handler's card on you?"

"Food handler's card?"

"Don't have one, huh?"

"Uh, not yet."

"Driver's license and social security cards, then. I hope you're not planning on sleeping on the beach, coming in here to clean up before your shift."

"No, I'll be looking for a place. I just hiked out . . . school just got out . . ."

Jeff's eyes narrowed. "You on the lam? Running from the law?"

"No," Romar said, sweat forming. If his uncle and aunt reported him missing, he could be running from the law. "I'm on summer break, I hiked out for a change from the city, I just finished tenth grade." Tenth sounded better than ninth, but the lie didn't come with a driver's license.

"Get a place, get yourself cleaned up, come back, we'll see," Jeff said. "I could use a night swamper. You know, mop floors, scrub toilets, clean kids fingerprints off windows."

Romar nodded, got to his feet and grabbed his pack.

"You sure you're not a runaway?" Jeff said, eyes narrowed. "I can't hire guys living on the beach, you see what I'm saying? And, we've all been warned about some guy that walked away from prison camp in North Bend. Authorities think he's headed north. But he's older. Forties, I think the flyer said."

"Yeah, quite a bit older. Thanks anyway." For the warning. He looked like a runaway. Maybe his picture was being circulated. The meth mouth werewolf dude back down the beach had to be the guy who wandered away from prison camp.

Three chances at a shot and he'd been pegged as homeless, an escaped prisoner, a runaway. Coach would bench him. Why had he stopped in Florence anyway? Because of Julie Matlock, who'd been nice to him. He was on a hike to find his mother and forgot all about her when another mother came along. A pretty blonde mother with a husband and two boys.

Those fries still smelled good, but he couldn't go back inside. He slogged on to a Grocery Outlet, grabbed a grocery cart and went on a shopping spree. Two apples, two oranges, two bananas, cheese slices, pepperoni, squeeze jar of mustard, day old hamburger buns, two big bottles of Mountain Dew, big bag of Red Vines. And a package of black socks, six pair for $2.99.

"Find everything you needed?" the checker asked.

"Yes ma'am, enough for lunch and dry feet." He stopped outside the store long enough to rip open the red vines bag with his teeth, and ate two at once. Then he opened the socks, managed to get a pair separated and onto his feet.

Driving rain drove him into a forest service campground six miles north of Florence. He used the restroom and checked out the place. A couple tents, one smoky fire, nothing that smelled like the guy back in the dunes. He set up his tent and built a fire with wood someone had stacked under a table. Pretty good, considering the rain. He rigged an aluminum windscreen from his dad's pack to reflect heat and dry his clothes and shoes.

Darkness came early where he'd set up under a thick stand of fir trees. Granny started talking in his head. *Think about that man on the beach. He must be the escaped prisoner. It's not just happenstance that two people*

you met today mentioned him. That one will be looking for money much as drink.
You put that money pouch I sewed onto your belt and you put your belt through your
pant loops. Sleep with your pants on. Keep your dad's knife handy.

Nor was it just happenstance that Granny talked in his head. He'd been holding the container with her ashes, thinking about how to say goodbye. His face felt wet. Darn rain. He put his money pouch on the too big belt and settled in his bag, Granny's ashes and his dad's knife clutched in his hands. Anyone who tried to take his granny or his money would get it in the gut.

5

VESTA'S BY THE SEA

Wednesday morning, gray soundless ocean, gray rain pelting his poncho, gray pavement, twenty miles to go before he could leave Granny's ashes at Smelt Sands Beach. Rain tapping on the poncho hood silenced the sound of passing vehicles until they were alongside him. The coast highway climbed and descended and climbed again. The climb tugged at back and calf muscles, the descent jabbed his knees. His shoes, semi-dry when he put them on, felt too tight, the second skin on his blisters too thin.

Five days ago he'd hiked out of Whitley's classroom, left a note for his Uncle Sherman and Aunt Joan, and wondered how far he'd get before someone found him and dragged him back to Roseburg. Maybe no one cared. He could hear Uncle Sherman say, "Let him go. He's big enough to take care of himself." Aunt Joan would agree. She'd never wanted him, or Granny either.

He hiked past the road to Sea Lion Caves with little sorrow about missing the animals. When they studied a map together, Granny pointed out the spot and told him you could smell them before you saw them. He paused long enough at Haceta Head Lighthouse viewpoint to eat what remained of his shopping spree. On the highway, vehicles whizzed past close enough to toss spray on his legs. Bicyclists pumped past on climbs, shot past fast as cars on descents, their heads down. One said, "Ciao, partner."

Those two words cut through the loneliness.

Three miles later, he used the restroom at a state park, filled his water bottles and stretched out atop a picnic table to rest his feet and shoulders. He adjusted his poncho to keep rain off his face, elevated his legs on his pack and let the falling rain lull him toward sleep. Colors whirled behind his closed eyelids like pinwheels twirling in the wind. He pictured waves washing Smelt Sands Beach as Granny described it and sensed her watching over him. In a way, she seemed to be walking with him, almost steering him, telling him to rest, take his time, he was far enough ahead of the smelly man who might be an escaped prisoner.

His pack felt like it gained another ten pounds while he rested. His feet throbbed with each heartbeat. Still ten or eleven miles to go. He thought about the last minutes in a close ball game and his coach shouting, "Focus on the basket. Keep your head in the game. Concentrate on the goal."

Determination kept him going until he smelled food. Hot food, like a roast in the oven. An old wood sign near the road edge read Vesta's by the Sea – Breakfast, Lunch, Groceries, RV Sites. The sign included a coffee cup with steam swirls below the words, but the steam coming out of the roof vent didn't smell like coffee. No amount of muttering "Only five or six miles, three hours at the most," kept him from crossing the parking lot and stepping onto the long covered porch. He stood there for a full minute to see if Granny would reach out, turn him around and give him a hard push.

Rain pounded the overhang, a pleasant sound when it wasn't drumming on his head. Faint music drifted from inside. He opened the door. A bell tinkled. He breathed in the aroma so deeply that his head spun and made him grab the door frame to keep from falling. His stomach growled.

A woman with gray hair swirling around her face like the pinwheels he'd seen behind his closed eyes looked up from behind a counter.

"Welcome, traveler. I've been expecting you. I'll bet you could use a bowl of my soup. Come in, have a seat." She turned a dial on the radio. The music stopped.

Romar pushed back the hood of his poncho. "I'm wet." Did the woman say she'd been expecting him? Or was that part of the dizzy spell? His stomach growled again, low at first, growing louder, like a watch dog when a stranger keeps coming at it.

The woman smiled. "And hungry. I heard that rumbling. This floor's accustomed to wet. The planks were once logs that floated up on the beach. Hang your cape on a hook by the door and lean your pack against the wall. I'll bring your soup and make a sandwich while you tell me why you're hiking in this weather."

"Uh, how much does it cost? Soup and sandwich?" He'd say no thanks, ask for an energy bar and get on his way.

"Not a penny. I only serve breakfast and lunch, and it's long past lunch time. It's been slow in here today. I knew someone would come along to help consume the leftovers. From the size of you, I'm betting you're the help I hoped for."

Hoped someone would come along, not expected him. He'd heard wrong. He hung his poncho on a hook without correcting the woman for calling it a cape. It dripped on the worn, uneven planks. A clock high above the woman's head showed it was going on five. He could still make Smelt Sands Beach before dark.

He sat at the first of four small tables, took off his glasses to dry them and felt them come apart in his hands. Rain and sweat had worked in under the tape. He set the right half on the table and squinted at the left half, tape jutting. Maybe he could scratch loose some sticky with a fingernail.

"Oh dear," the woman said, "we'll need to find some new black tape. Or better yet, a frame the right size for the glass." The woman set down a huge bowl of steaming soup and a basket of assorted crackers. "Vegetable beef, more beef than vegetable. Eat a few crackers while I make you a sandwich."

She returned a few minutes later with a sandwich of thick sliced whole wheat bread, stacked meat, lettuce and tomato, and a glass of milk. "Milk goes well with a meat sandwich. Take your coffee or tea after to help your food digest. Which will it be?"

"Tea," he said. He'd often had tea with his granny.

"I'll bring my tea and join you. You can tell me about your journey."

"I need to make it to the town called Yachats today," he said, noticing her unusual eyes peering over small glasses. Almost yellow like a cat's. "Smelt Sands Beach, actually."

"Another six miles." She placed a mug of tea and a cup of soup on the table and sat across from him. "Tomorrow will be soon enough. Unless someone is waiting for you there."

Romar settled back in his chair and stretched his long legs toward the window wall. His feet burned, his calf muscles tightened. He flexed his toes. "Not really. I'm sort of stopping off there for awhile. I'm on my way north . . . to Washington."

The woman leaned her head left and smiled again. Her eyes went greenish in the dim light. "I'm Vesta. What name shall I call you?"

He considered saying Andrew, his middle name, but something about the woman made him want to be honest. "Romar. It's kind of odd." He'd consumed most of the soup and wolfed down half the sandwich.

"Yes," she said, "Romar is an unusual name, though I've heard it before. Do you have a summer job in Yachats? At one of the restaurants or inns?"

"Not really. I tried to get a restaurant job in Florence to earn a little extra money, but I don't have a food handler's card." Why he told her that he didn't know. Somehow, when he looked at her, he saw Granny, though they looked nothing alike. She kept smiling and words kept spilling out of his mouth. "Would there be a job near Smelt Sands Beach? I might want to stay close by there for a time."

"It's a very small beach. All of Yachats is close by."

"My grandmother grew up at the beach. I'm delivering some of her ashes. My dad was supposed to take them there when she died, but he got killed, so she had me promise I'd see to it." He leaned across the table, eyes squinted, to watch the woman's face. "Will the town mind, do you think? Leaving some of her at the beach, I mean."

"I doubt the town will know, unless you tell someone."

"Oh," he said, chewing on that thought along with a bite of sandwich. "Well, I just told you."

"I keep my own counsel. Tell me more about your grandmother."

"She left the ocean when she married my grandfather. He logged and worked in mills around Roseburg. She saw to me until she died." He stared at his empty soup bowl, eyes wide to stop tears.

The woman took the bowl and pushed away from the table. "I'll bring you some more soup."

"Thank you Mrs. Vesta," he said.

She laughed. It sounded like the bell that tinkled when he opened the door. "Vesta is my given name. No Mrs. necessary." She set the filled bowl in front of him. A chunk of beef poked a couple inches above the broth. He knew she'd dipped up the biggest pieces for him.

He looked right at the lights in her eyes. "Granny wouldn't like me using your given name. She taught me better."

Again the woman nodded. "Well, then, it's Mrs. Palmateer, but everyone from two years old on up calls me Vesta. It means goddess of the hearth. When I hear my name, I feel like the speaker is calling me Goddess, which sounds much nicer than Mrs."

Romar felt a smile stretching his cheeks and around his eyes. It must have been the first time he'd smiled that day. Maybe the first time since saying goodbye to Julie Matlock. He missed her.

"Thank you Goddess Vesta. Other than my granny, only a goddess could make soup this good."

Vesta kept talking to him, asking him questions, getting honest answers from him before he could come up with lies. He looked at the clock. Twelve minutes after six.

"You meant to be on your way, and I've kept you talking," Vesta said, "so I have a suggestion. Spend the night and continue your journey in the morning. There's a caretaker's room downstairs at the back of the building. A bed where you can roll out your sleeping bag or crawl in under the covers. Nothing fancy, but it's warm. The furnace is a bit noisy. It's downstairs, too. And showers and laundry room for the RV park. There's only a couple campers parked for the night. Now and then a rig pulls in after I close. Pay no attention if that happens."

Romar knew he should thank her and be on his way, but his big head started flopping up and down, nodding yes. A bed. A furnace. A shower. He dug in his pack for his Rec Specs so he could focus on the woman's face while he offered to do some work, whatever the caretaker might do. He was pulling the specs elastic band over his head when Vesta spoke again.

"We can talk in the morning over an early breakfast. I start before six, so I'm ready to clean up here and put my feet up for the night. I'll tell you more about the caretaker's job, just in case you decide to stay in the area for a time. You could visit Smelt Sands Beach often."

Romar got his specs in place and got to his feet. "Why are you being so nice to me? I mean, you don't know me, I just walked in off the highway. I could be that escaped prisoner they're looking for down in Florence."

Vesta looked up at him. "There's a good chance I might know that escaped prisoner. You're not him. I'm a very good judge of character. And I wouldn't need my sixth sense to know you're tired, you'd like to soak your feet and rest in a warm, dry place." She went around behind the counter, opened a drawer, handed him a looped rope with two keys. "There's a short stairway on the north side of the building. It's well lighted. The door you want says Private. You'll be comfortable."

"I can help you clean up here. Wash the dishes or sweep the floor."

"Thank you, Romar. I'll take care of things tonight. You can help wash dishes and sweep tomorrow. And tell me the rest of your story."

A shiver started low on his back, climbed to his neck and lifted the hair on his arms. He stood on the porch twirling the keys. He could hang them on the door and walk away from Vesta's kindness and strange eyes. Hike on in deafening rain and dreary grayness. Or he could sleep on a bed, eat a good breakfast, wash a few dishes and head out. Either way, if she'd figured him out and called the police, they'd find him. He hefted his pack onto one arm and walked down the steps.

A security light came on as he stepped onto the landing. He startled, caught in the glare, and back-pedaled one step. Raindrops caught the light, intensifying the grayness beyond the building. He could hear the sea. When he moved again, another light blinked on, this one above the door marked Private.

He covered the distance in three giant steps, fumbled with the key and half fell inside when the door swung open. A hooked rug in front of the door reminded him of one Granny made. So did the quilt on the bed and the things covering the armrests of a recliner and sofa. Washable covers, that's what Granny called them.

Sea shells and books filled a tall narrow bookcase and the shelf under an old TV. A vase in the center of a round maple table on the kitchen side of the room held flowers that looked like sweet peas.

"Granny?" he whispered. He felt her there. Did that make him crazy? Or just tired?

6

YACHATS (AT THE FOOT OF THE MOUNTAIN)

Romar wakened to footfalls overhead, the furnace rumbling beyond the wall, music from the radio he'd set before falling into bed. A brightness shown at the windows, one by the bed, the other by the kitchen table. Not quite sunny, but no rain.

He showered, dressed and headed upstairs. At the top he halted, as if someone barked an order, to look at the scene across the highway. A forest stretched north and south, every shade of green, some trees almost black. The day before he'd walked head down, eyes focused on the highway, the ocean on his left, and on his mind. He'd forgotten about the Coast Range, the national forest Granny said was at Yachats' back door.

We should have gone out to Smelt Sands Beach before your dad was killed. He would have loved seeing all the old spruce trees.

He looked around for Granny, her voice had been that clear, then stepped onto the long plank porch. Vesta opened the cafe door before he reached for the handle, led him to a table where steaming plates waited, one heaped far higher than the other. Ham, scrambled eggs, fried potatoes, a plate with stacked toast already buttered. Glasses of milk and orange juice, a pot of hot coffee, another of hot water, tea bags, empty cups.

"There's a forest across the street," he said.

"Yes. Cummins Creek Wilderness, to be precise. Take a seat."

He let out a breath that sounded like "Ah," and sat. "My dad was a river and trail guide on the North Umpqua. My granny was his mother."

"Yes, your dad was meant to bring your granny's ashes out to the beach. I remember. We'll have a bite or two before I turn on the open sign. Maybe talk a bit about your granny before you hold your private service for her. What was her maiden name?"

"Esther Jarvi," Romar said, food on its way to his mouth. How could he be so hungry after all she'd fed him the night before?

"There are Jarvi family members in Yachats," Vesta said. "You could meet them, if you stay on a few days. I could use some help, tomorrow especially. There's an old bike you can ride for your trip to Smelt Sands, though you'll have to push it part of the way up the cape."

"A Jarvi family?" He set down his fork, grabbed a piece of toast and worked on what that could mean. Granny never said much about the family she'd left behind when she married his grandfather and moved to Glide. At least he didn't remember much, not like he remembered her talking about the beach, catching smelt in her hands, chasing waves.

"You'll find the Jarvi name on graves at the far north side of the cemetery. It's right along the highway. You'll see it on your way. Go up near the top to have a look."

Something in her eyes told him she had more information about the family with that name, but he kept on eating rather than ask. When he finished, she told him where to find the bike and, just like that, the decision was made. He'd borrow her bike for the trip with Granny's ashes, and then he'd return to spend another night.

The bike was an old but still good ten-speed that made it almost to the top of the long climb to Cape Perpetua before refusing to go another inch no matter how much energy he put into pushing on the pedals. When he started hiking again, he'd stop at the cape long enough to check out the overlook, the highest point on the Oregon coast. He'd learned that from a book Vesta handed him.

"Yachats means 'at the foot of the mountain,'" she said. "Your granny grew up on the ocean at the foot of the mountain." He liked that.

He geared down for the descent. If Granny was with him in spirit, he wanted her to enjoy the trip across the Yachats River and through the town. He spotted the small sign that pointed to Smelt Sands Beach, pushed the bike to a bench and took in the view that his granny grew up seeing every day. He heard her voice in his head so clearly he wondered how often she'd spoken the same words.

Waves pounded against the basalt along the shore just north of where we had our little house. Spray and foam shot into the air. Wind carried it onto the rocks where it slid back into the sea.. Right in front of our place, the waves washed in and tumbled tiny rocks that came down from the mountain oh so long ago. Smelt spawned there, in that one small place. We caught them in our hands.

He chained the bicycle to a nearby bench and carried Granny's ashes onto the tumbled rocks. They glistened even without full sun, just like those she kept in a jar in the window sill in Glide. He spotted tiny golden agates and dark lava chips. The beach was tucked into a small cove created and protected by an eroding sandstone wall. It would be the marker stone for his small portion of Granny's ashes.

After fifteen minutes of watching waves wash over and tumble the small rocks, Romar had a clear sense of what would happen when he let Granny's ashes go. The lightest might float on the waves for a time. Soon, all would settle amongst the rocks. He liked the idea that some might be heavy enough to stay right there to get covered so that he could find part of her whenever he returned for a visit. Tears ran down his cheeks.

He waded out knee deep, unmindful of the cold water, and released the contents of the plastic container into a wave crest that soaked his thighs. "Goodbye, Granny. I hope you and my dad are together in spirit land." He felt heat flush his chest and face, and dry his tears. Back above the water line he filled the container with rock chips, vowing to keep them forever and ever, Amen.

With that promise and prayer, he braved the cemetery and found Jarvi headstones. Names that must have been Granny's relatives, and therefore his, didn't mean a thing until he came on one with a birth date close to Granny's and a death date ten years back. Edmund Jarvi, 1927 to 1998. Granny talked now and then about her cousin, Eddie. Romar remembered the day he came home from kindergarten to find her crying. She'd wiped her tears and said, "Eddie's gone. My cousin, more like a big brother. That's about it for the Jarvi name. None of them seemed able to produce sons."

He'd asked where Eddie had gone. She said to heaven, and explained about earthly remains going into the ground, souls to heaven. They'd visited a cemetery so he could understand the place that held earthly remains.

That night he heard her tell his dad to have her cremated so she wouldn't be trapped in the ground. She'd wanted all her ashes set free at Smelt Sands Beach, but Uncle Sherman had other ideas. Most of Granny's ashes were trapped in a container in Roseburg Cemetery. He had a rush of anger at his uncle. Why couldn't Sherman have been more like Roland? Or like their mother, his granny?

Romar knelt down in front of Edmund Jarvi's headstone like he'd seen people do in movies. There must be some reason for doing that. Otherwise, why bother with cemeteries and headstones?

"Hey, Eddie, can you hear me?" he whispered. "Or did you go by Ed? Or Edmund? Did you see me just now? Out on the beach with Granny's ashes? She's your cousin, the one you called Essie. If you get this message, you can help me decide if I should stay around Yachats for awhile before I try to find my mother."

He didn't hear a sound, not one word but, a mind-picture of Edmund playing basketball in high school flitted into his brain. Edmund's face looked a lot like his own. So did Edmund's long legs and baggy uniform. In spite of determination not to cry over anything less than his granny, tears leaked out and puddled in his Rec Specs. He pulled the frame away from his face, let the tears snake down his cheeks like they had out on the beach and mopped them up with his shirt sleeve.

When no clearer message came, he headed south to Vesta's. She might know something about Edmund Jarvi, like whether his ghost floated around the Yachats cemetery in an old basketball uniform.

The aroma of cooking meat drifted on the air from Vesta's By the Sea just as it had the evening before and, like then, set off a major rumble in his stomach. It took all the will he could muster to park the bike in the garage, not just jump off and dash inside. He stashed his container of agates and other small rocks in the caretaker's room, washed up and took the stairs three at a time.

"Meatloaf," Vesta said when he opened the door. "With oven fried potatoes and green beans. I knew you'd need something hearty after your trip."

Romar pulled off his Rec Specs, almost opaque with salt spray on the outside and tear salt on the inside. He breathed in until his head spun. His grumbling stomach sounded like Granny's washer when it had a load off kilter. He grabbed the waiting fork before his backside landed in the chair and didn't really look at a man hunched over the far table until half the meatloaf slab got his stomach/washer agitating properly. The man spoke when Romar looked up.

"Move down here when you've filled your belly, lad. I've got your broken specs."

Romar squinted as tight as he could to bring the man into focus but saw only a blur. He held his salty specs to his eyes and saw a craggy face with a fluff of white hair that looked like feathers. The man's table was covered with glass frames, pliers and a hair dryer with a cup attached to the blower. He wore aviator glasses.

Vesta said, "Romar Jones, meet Ian Gallagher, an old friend of mine."

"Old optician," the man said. "We're going to fix you up with some decent frames soon as you pick a pair that will take your lenses without too much filing and fuss."

Romar, still busy cramming meatloaf and potatoes into his mouth, looked from Vesta to the optician and back. A starved dog would have better manners. That came straight from Granny. He worked to get a mouthful properly chewed and swallowed, and said, "Pleased to meet you, sir."

"Ian'll do. Don't rush yourself and get a bellyache. I've got plenty enough time and Vesta's got plenty enough coffee and cookies fresh out of the oven."

Vesta delivered another thick slice of meatloaf and more potatoes to his plate. "Eat your beans before you start on this serving of meat."

"You sound like my granny." He ate all the beans, cleaned his plate, drank a tall glass of milk in one long swallow and headed for the sink behind the counter.

"I'll take those things. You sit down and get acquainted with Ian. We can't have you wearing those goggle specs when you're tending to customers."

He sat, mouth open to explain why he needed to get back to his hike, blood too busy digesting food to let his brain work. Or maybe his brain was working. Why go looking for a mother in prison when he could work for a goddess who shoved glass frames out of the way to set a plate of chocolate chip cookies in front of him?

"Now, here's the thing," Ian Gallagher said between bites of cookie and sips of coffee. "Your correction's a strong one and the material used in your lenses is an old standard, not the new polycarbonate. That limits what we can do with a frame until you get a new prescription." He put down his coffee mug and picked up one half of Romar's broken frame, now without a lens in it. " But we can come up with something better than these sorry-looking things you've been wearing. Vesta, sweetheart, can you bring us a mirror?"

Ian Gallagher leaned across the table, frames aimed at Romar's face and next thing he knew he was squinting at his reflection in Vesta's mirror. He needed to say "No thanks," but his mouth didn't work any better than his brain. The only thing working was his stuffed stomach, where digestive juices squirted in to churn meatloaf and potatoes and beans into usable nutrients. Coach explained how that worked. Blood for muscles so they wouldn't cramp, blood for the brain to think about the best shot. Basketball required thinking. So did this situation.

"The right glasses can make the man, so to speak. Make a difference." Ian Gallagher talked about the frame heater that looked like a hair dryer, and how lens grooves could be filed a bit here and frames tinkered with a bit there.

The third frame, one that didn't look thick enough to hold glass, looked good. Romar leaned closer to the mirror, turning his head to clear the astigmatism blur.

"How . . . how much is this one?" He could hang around, earn a few bucks, enough to pay for his meals plus the frames.

"Nada. All these frames retired along with me when I closed shop and took up fishing. Clam digging. Walking the beach after a good storm." Ian fiddled with the frame and Romar's lenses.

"Granny wouldn't like me accepting so many favors. Meals. The room. Now these frames."

Ian lowered his head and squinted over the top of his glasses. "Vesta's hoping you'll stick around. Take over the caretaker job for the summer. She considers you family since your grandmother was a Jarvi." He looked at Vesta. "Am I right, sweetheart?"

"He's right," Vesta said, her eyes on Romar. "Would you consider it? Some inside work behind the counter, some outside work with a lawn mower and weed eater. Some down on your hands and knees weeding out flower beds."

"Well . . ."

"I know you want to get to Washington, to your mother, but you said she's not expecting you."

He shifted in his chair, trying to find a comfortable spot, one not nail-sharp with lies and unspoken truths. "Well, no, but . . . well . . . there's a lot you don't know about me."

"I know enough. You hiked out here from Roseburg to honor your grandmother's wishes. She was a Jarvi. Yachats could use another Jarvi for certain."

That odd light she had in the center of her eyes burned into Romar's brain. It felt kind of warm, not so scary as the night before. "I'd sort of like a job. I could use the money to keep going. Keep eating, mostly. It might take some time to figure out a few things. Like, what to say when I find the address."

After another prod from Granny, who seemed to be listening in, he added, "See, my mother's in prison. I'm not sure how to get in. To visit, I mean."

He watched Vesta's eyes, certain that news would make her lower her head or turn away. Most people did. Kids whispered, most of the time loud enough so he knew what they said. *His mother's a criminal.* But Vesta smiled and nodded like she'd known that all along.

"It's settled, then. I've learned a bit about visiting inside jail. It calls for some planning ahead."

He pushed at the empty frames. They sat square on his nose and pushing didn't help him see any better.

Vesta put her hand on his arm. "Meals, room and a fair wage.

We'll work out the details when mister fix-it here isn't eavesdropping. He doesn't need to know all our business. Do we have a deal?"

Romar nodded, swallowed, whispered, "Yes."

She handed him a pamphlet about a food handler's card. "Study this so you'll be ready for the test."

"Test?" he said, and knew he should tell her about walking out of school. Instead, he grabbed a chocolate chip cookie from the plate she held right under his nose.

7

CARETAKER BY THE SEA

He got to work the next morning determined to earn his keep – make his own way in the world like Uncle Sherman had been saying he should for two years. The job his uncle had in mind meant summers in Medford working for Aunt Arlene. With Granny gone, Uncle Sherman and Aunt Joan might decide to leave him in Medford straight through school until he graduated. They hadn't said that, but he worried about it.

Vesta led him through the grocery store/gift shop section of her business, explaining how she wanted shelves, coolers and freezers stocked. She showed him the cleaning closet and supplies she kept upstairs, and said the restroom needed to be checked every hour once customers started using it.

"Got it," he said.

The kitchen routine seemed easy enough: carry food Vesta prepared to tables, refill coffee cups, wash pots and pans too large for the dishwasher.

When the first rush was over, Vesta said, "Grab another bite and take a broom to the front porch." She narrowed her eyes and added, "That means sweep it, not just carry a broom out there and prop it against the wall like my last caretaker took to doing."

"Yes ma'am. Vesta." She was the coach, sending him into the game. He swept porch sand onto the parking strip where wind caught it and blew some back where it came from. So, wind and sand made up the opposing team.

Two cars pulled in while he worked. A couple wandered over from the RV park. He got the sand in check and went inside to wash up.

"Grab an apron from the cleaning closet," Vesta said.

An apron? He scrubbed his hands, splashed water on his face, just in case, and checked his new glasses in the mirror. They looked good. He dropped the apron loop over his head and went to the kitchen side of the counter to check out how team Vesta wore the uniform.

She glanced at him and grinned. "That'll wrap around those slender hips twice." She grabbed the dangling strings, wrapped and tied, and patted his arm. "Coffee refills all around, ask if they'd like anything else, another car's pulling in, wash your hands a lot and take your cues from me."

Coffee refills were easy shots, one point each. Stacking and removing dirty dishes and silver required some finesse – two points per trip. Vesta cooked extra bacon and scrambled eggs for an order, and tucked a filled plate in a spot where he could eat without being seen. Slam dunk breakfast.

He caught on to liquid butter and a brush for toast, four slices at a time, a couple for himself. He poured a little coffee into a mug of hot chocolate for the caffeine, and mastered stacking plates, glasses, mugs and silver in the dishwasher.

After ten-thirty, most orders were for coffee and muffins or rolls. Easy orders but customers left crumbs, crumpled napkins and wrappers on tables, sand on the floor. He wiped off tables and swept while Vesta started lunch – clam chowder and deli sandwiches she made, hard rolls and fresh cookies dropped off by a bakery delivery van.

By the time Vesta closed the kitchen at three, Romar had taken several breaks, apron removed, to help guide motor homes and trailers into the park. He'd rung up sales at the grocery counter, adding items in his head along with the computerized cash register, checking it for accuracy against his own math. Maybe it should have been the other way around, checking his accuracy against the computer, but he trusted himself more. If he'd been half as good at poetry as at math, he'd be in Roseburg High waiting for the last bell, worrying about being sent to Medford.

School. Had his uncle and aunt called the office to tell them he'd taken off? Word would have gotten around whether they called or not. Josh Mobley could've stopped by the office to report giving him a ride.

An adrenalin rush made his legs and arms jumpy. He took deep breaths to get his heart rate back under control. Shelves, coolers and the freezer needed restocking. He concentrated on the task, old stock forward, new back. He needed to tell Vesta the truth, but she needed him to sweep out the shelter, lay a fire in the pit and bring more firewood from the dungeon.

"Wood disappears if we leave too much in the shelter. Folks wander up from the beach to help themselves." She handed him a set of keys marked Rest Rooms, Laundry, Dungeon. "Sweep the steps down to the beach, too, then chase a wave. It's coming on five and you haven't had a break all day. We'll have help tomorrow. My niece." She poked a pen into her pinwheel hair and smiled.

He'd tell her the truth over the weekend. For sure before school got out in Roseburg. By then he'd have earned a little more money. Maybe enough to take a bus if she kicked him out. Hiking alone along highways wasn't all that great. Or camping without his dad.

Vesta's by the Sea was an old vertical log building with its top floor at highway level, its lower floor set into the hillside that sloped toward the beach. The caretaker's apartment, rest rooms and laundry had windows facing the ocean. The furnace/storage/tool room behind them had no windows. It did feel like a dungeon. Would the name be a metaphor?

The RV park was laid out in three tiers, with a gravel path to the shelter — an open structure with a cement floor and circular brick fire pit in the center. Screens hung from a metal shield attached to the flue pipe. He arranged tables and benches around the fire pit, carried a couple redwood chairs out to the lawn where guests could see the ocean, then swept the steps leading to the beach. Nails poked up out of the hand rail. He stashed the broom, grabbed a hefty hammer, tended to the nails and headed for the beach, hammer still in hand. The stairs ended on a rocky patch with a wide stretch of sand beyond.

To the south he saw driftwood pieces standing on end, scrap lumber perched on top and part of a blue tarp flapping in the breeze.

He jumped across a stream that trickled through the rocks and ran toward the makeshift camp, arms tucked close to his sides, hammer in his right hand, a heavy rock in his left. He lifted them, as if they were weights, to work his biceps. As he approached the makeshift camp he saw duct tape held tarp pieces together. A battered aluminum pot nested in charred wood in a rock-surrounded fire pit. A plastic bucket rested upside down on a piece of driftwood. The dense brush behind the camp reeked of careless camping, or worse.

The brush rustled. Romar scanned the bank, saw branches move, saw a human form, eyes watching him. His senses told him he'd seen the man before. Dirty, smelly man with rotten breath seeking drink or smoke. The man he'd dubbed Meth Mouth. He raised his right arm toward the brush, pounded air with his hammer, turned and sprinted for Vesta's.

Could the man he'd seen in the dunes travel that far in four days? Only if he'd hitched a ride. "Holy damn," Romar said, the only expletive he'd ever heard his dad use. The camp stood just beyond the southern edge of Vesta's RV Park. Kids playing on the beach would head for it. They liked forts. He had to tell Vesta. She'd probably alert the forest service or some other authority.

Authority as in police. "Double damn." He might as well turn himself in right then. He sprinted in loose sand, feeling the burn in his calves and lungs, ran up the steps, saw guests in the shelter, fire burning. They'd need more wood. He stopped in the caretaker's room long enough for a quick clean-up so he'd look halfway civil when he told Vesta the truth.

"Romar," she said when he opened the door to her cafe and store, "I need that last tray of sandwiches from the walk-in. Then help Ian in the grocery section. The park's full. A caravan pulled in. Six rigs traveling together. They're the ones burning up all the wood in the shelter."

It took a couple beats for him to understand she meant the RV park. The smile she gave him brought an ache to his chest. Customers standing in front of the deli case smiled too.

They stayed busy long past Vesta's nine o'clock closing time. That's when Romar, who'd mentally practiced a speech, blurted,

"There's a fetid camp south of here. Must be just beyond your boundary. Up against the bank, into the bushes."

"Fetid?" Ian Gallagher said. "As in malodorous?"

"Uh, yeah." Romar wondered what happened to the speech he'd planned and why he'd said fetid. Whitley must have used the word for some guy's stinky poem. "I think it's the same guy I saw in the dunes."

"Who?" Ian asked, eyebrows raised above his cool glasses.

Romar didn't answer the who question. He wanted to get it the whole story out in the open and deal with what came next. "He thought I'd have something to drink in my pack. Or smokes, at least. I told him I'm an athlete and underage. You know I'm under drinking age. Right?"

Vesta and Ian both frowned. The center of Vesta's eyes glowed red, a reflection from the closed sign. That's when he figured it out — she'd had one of those surgeries where the eye doctor puts a lens in the person's eyes.

"Right," Vesta said.

"But not how far under. You didn't ask so I didn't tell you, not that it's your fault, I don't mean that, it's my fault and my granny wants the matter cleared up. I hear her saying so in my head." He had his eyes on Vesta's. "I'm only fifteen and a half, I walked out of school and packed up my gear and headed out here with Granny's ashes and plans to make it to Washington to find my mother and I would have kept on walking right past here but for the smell coming out of your place. The food smell. And then you were so nice . . ."

He turned to face Ian. "And then you were so nice too, and I thought I could stay for awhile and not say anything. Until I checked out that camp and smelled that man. It's all about smells working on my brain and Granny reminding me how I grew up, that I'm not like my mother, but that smelly man on the beach might be. Like her, I mean. A criminal. That man could be the escaped prisoner the restaurant people in Florence heard about. He could be on meth, which makes people crazy. See, the awful smell coming from him isn't just from . . . from going in the woods, if you know what I mean. It's from rotting teeth and really bad breath. Meth mouth bad, which I think my mother's must have been one time when my Uncle Sherman and Aunt Joan saw her. Not that they ever told me anything, I just overheard

Aunt Joan, so I read about meth online at the library. The guy on the beach could be cooking in a battered soup pot over a beach fire." He dragged in a breath. "So, I'd better pack up and get out of here before I get you in trouble along with myself."

Vesta moved to him, wrapped her plump arms around him and squeezed, stepped back, her hands on his arms. "Oh, Romie, you're not going anywhere." The tears he tried to keep hidden burned his eyelids. One tear snuck out, ran under his Ian Gallagher-crafted glasses and slid down the side of his nose. The room spun upside down; he sagged like a stack of soggy locker room towels when one too many landed on the pile. His head pounded.

Ian crouched beside him, lifted an eyelid, checked his pulse. Then Vesta crouched too, a glass of juice in one hand, a plate of food in the other. The two of them exchanged looks that spoke words he couldn't read.

"You poor boy, you haven't eaten a bite since lunch, we've been so busy."

His stomach growled. He downed the juice, took a bite of sandwich, resisted Ian's attempt to get him back on his feet.

"Come on, Romar, let's get you up and properly seated on a chair. Don't you think he'd be more comfortable at a table, sweetheart?"

"Floor's fine. Great. It's a great floor. Built from planks that floated in on the waves, right?"

"I told him that," Vesta said. "Help me get him up. We need to hear more about his uncle and aunt."

He set down the sandwich, pushed himself up, grabbed the sandwich again and headed for the tables. Truth time wasn't over.

"Your aunt and uncle," Vesta said. "Were you living with them? Before you packed up and left Roseburg?"

"Uh, yeah."

"So, they're your legal guardians?"

He put his sandwich on the table but remained standing. *Stand up straight and tell the truth.*

"Right. Uncle Sherman's my dad's brother. He's my legal guardian, but it's not like I'm a welfare case. There was some money from my dad. Granny saw to me all my life, but Uncle Sherman took over everything after my dad was killed. That's when we moved to Roseburg. Granny and me. Uncle Sherman and Aunt Joan wouldn't let us stay in Glide. They sold our house."

Vesta was frowning again. "Does your uncle know where you are?"

"Sort of."

Ian Gallagher laid a hand on Vesta's arm, but his narrowed eyes were on Romar. "Wait a minute. I'm trying to catch up with this story. Your dad was killed, your mother's in prison in Washington, your grandmother who saw to you died recently, you're fifteen and a half, and you walked out of school in Roseburg and stopped off here by chance?"

Romar nodded. "Because I smelled food."

"And I'm trying to find out if his legal guardian knows where he is," Vesta said.

"Okay, sweetheart, okay. You're right, that's important. Romar, does your guardian know where you are?"

"I left them a note. That said I was going to Washington to look for my mother."

"Have you called them since you left Roseburg?" Ian asked.

Romar sighed. "No. But I don't think they're worried. They're probably glad to have me gone."

Vesta's hands settled on her hips. "We need to call right now. Though it's a little late. Ten-thirty on a Friday night. Do you think he'd still be up, Romie?"

Romie. He considered that a good sign. "They're probably not home this early, they like to stay in town on Friday nights."

"When their nephew is missing? I don't think so." Vesta grabbed the phone. "If they're not home, we'll leave a message so they can call back."

"Uh . . ." Romar felt like he'd tripped over his feet at mid-court and the other team grabbed the ball and scored. Sweat ran down his sides. He probably smelled worse than Meth Mouth.

"Whoa whoa whoa," Ian said. "Hold on a minute, sweetheart. Let's think this through. Get some more info. Maybe make a couple other calls first."

"To whom, may I ask?" The laser lights in Vesta's eyes could have sliced a ball into sections on its way to the basket.

"Contacts of mine who can check out a few things. Find out if we've got a missing person or a runaway teen, there's a world of difference, believe me." He took off his glasses and rubbed the bridge of his nose.

"Oh." Vesta put the phone down, and pulled out a chair to sit.

Romar released his breath and picked up his sandwich.

"Which is it?" Vesta said. "Missing person or runaway teen?"

"Chances are, he wouldn't know, sweetheart. That would depend on what his uncle reported. Let's sit down, make a few notes, think this through."

"Maybe I should leave before I cause any more trouble."

"Trust me on this — Vesta doesn't want you to leave, and I want you to sit back down."

Romar sat. Ian collected names, starting with Mr. Whitley, leaving spaces for addresses and phone numbers. He jotted down a timeline and soon had notes on Romar's route and everyone he'd encountered along the way, from Josh Mobley on.

The clock hands reached eleven, ten after, a quarter after. Then Ian asked a couple dozen questions about Uncle Sherman and Aunt Joan, and shook his head over and over.

"All right, that's enough for now," Ian said. "Vesta, sweetheart, here's what I want you to remember. Kids who feel loved and wanted do not run away from home. You and I have talked about that. Am I right, Romar? About the loved and wanted part?"

Romar looked at his hands, one still holding the last of his sandwich, dry and hard. He'd never expected love from his uncle and aunt, but he thought they should love Granny. Uncle Sherman, at least, since she was his mother.

"My uncle and aunt didn't want Granny and me, but it was the right thing to do. I never blamed them any. I mean, like Aunt Joan said, they'd just gotten their two daughters out of the house, and then along we came, two more people to cook for and clean up after. Lots more laundry with my sports and stuff."

"So your aunt had all the responsibility for meal preparation and housework?" Vesta asked.

Romar shook his head. "Granny cooked for all of us until the day she died. I helped her with the housework. I kept up the yard, the outdoor stuff."

"So, in fact, your aunt has only had cooking and housework responsibility since your granny died, right?"

"More or less," Romar said. "Mostly, after Granny died, we ate take-out. Granny taught me how to do laundry a long time ago, so I took care of my own. But, you know, there's a lot of wear and tear on the linens, like all the towels and stuff, so it got to be a burden for Aunt Joan."

Vesta pushed herself away from the table. "Dear God, Romie, you don't mean to tell me your aunt complained about you using towels?"

She stretched the word into ows and ohs, dips and rises. He nodded because it was true. His aunt complained about towels and sheets and extra detergent to keep up with extra laundry.

Ian said, "Take it easy, sweetheart. And take a little brandy before you crawl into bed."

He turned to Romar. "Look, son, you've found a place where you're welcome and respected, but it's been an odd day. I need your word that you'll go downstairs, get some sleep, and be back up here to help Vesta in the morning. No walking out this door, grabbing your pack and taking off."

Romar shook his head, then nodded, not certain if he should answer 'Yes' or 'No', too tired to care right then if authorities showed up in the night and dragged him from Vesta's caretaker's bed. "If I'm still welcome as caretaker . . ."

"Good," Ian said. "Let's all get some sleep. See what tomorrow brings."

Romar stumbled downstairs to the caretaker's room. He knew what tomorrow would bring. He'd have to call Uncle Sherman and Aunt Joan. Among other things, he'd have to admit he'd never intended to get shuttled off to Aunt Arlene in Medford.

8

VESTA'S NIECE

Fog, that's what the day brought. Fog drifted in off the ocean, swirled around trees and buildings and settled in Romar's head, muddling his thoughts. What would he say to his uncle?

He set the four tables for Vesta's breakfast customers. She could be in trouble for harboring a fugitive. Worrying made his head pound like the waves pounded the rocky headland south of Vesta's.

The door chimes sounded. A woman's voice said, "Good morning, Auntie V. Sorry we're late."

The woman headed for the kitchen, veered off toward him like a point guard driving the key, put her open hand on his forearm and squeezed. "Auntie V's right, you are a hunk."

"Hunk?" Hand on arm. Personal foul.

The woman squeezed again. Her hair, some black, some gray, bunched up on her shoulders. Earrings made of colored glass tangled with her hair in a way that must hurt her head when she tried to sort it out.

"I said handsome, not hunk, you know I don't use that word." Vesta poured a mug of coffee and set it on the counter. "Where's Kyra?"

"She went out to the beach to pay homage to the sun god. Or to chase off the fog, I'm not sure which."

"Well, then, permit me to make introductions. Leila, meet Romar. Romar, this is my niece, Leila."

Romar took Leila's offered hand. "Good morning, ma'am," he said, and noticed colored glass dangling from her wrist. More colored glass plunged into her cleavage, a word he'd learned before he'd been tall enough to look down into any. He averted his eyes. Granny would be upset if he stared.

"We had a busy night last night," Vesta said. "I could use some help this side of the counter soon as you're through flirting with my caretaker."

When the door chime sounded again, Romar forgot all about the woman's cleavage and Granny's warnings. A pretty girl with straight blonde hair halfway to her waist darted past him, threw her arms around Vesta and kissed her cheek. He noticed her eyes as she went by, the bluest eyes he'd ever seen. He noticed the rest of her, too. He'd bet his big hands could circle her waist. Big, sweaty hands that he wiped down his apron.

"Auntie Gram, I'm starved," the girl said.

"You're always starved, Kyra, dear." Vesta went through introductions again, explained that Kyra was Leila's daughter and her grandniece. "And a grand girl she is."

The girl smiled at him. "Hello. I'm so glad Auntie Gram found a new caretaker. We've been worried about her out here all by herself. You never know when kooks are going to wander out of the woods or off the beach." She did something with her eyes like he'd seen girls do in school; something one girl told him meant older people didn't get it. He'd said, "Get what?" Not his brightest moment.

"Kooks?" His voice sounded like he had his mouth full of marshmallows.

"Weirdoes," she said.

"Like meth heads?" He thought about the guy down the beach and wondered if Vesta had mentioned that whole story to this woman and girl.

Kyra nodded. "They're the worst. I'm sure Vesta's last caretaker was into something, but we never found out what."

"Let it go, Kyra," Vesta said.

At the same time her mother said, "Don't go there."

Vesta and Leila tossed eye signals across the kitchen. He could see them, up and over the net like a volleyball. Kyra laughed. "You two, you're about as subtle as Auntie Gram's emergency air horn going off in the middle of the night."

The eye signals stopped. The door opened on a noisy group. In less than two minutes, all four tables had people sipping coffee or hot chocolate, and reading menus. A man from the RV Park came in, looked around and asked if he could carry an order down to the picnic tables in the shelter. An order for five people. He had a list in his hand.

"Set up three tables, Romar" Vesta said. "Plastic table cloths from the storage room. Slip on the clips stored with them or the cloths will end up out on the highway. You may need to sweep the floor again. Get a new fire going." She handed him a fireplace lighter.

Romar clutched table cloths, clips and lighter to his chest, glad to leave the indoor chores for the women. He couldn't wait to get outside, though he missed every one of them before the door closed behind him. He swept away what little sand had blown into the shelter, clipped cloths on tables and straightened benches.

A foghorn sounded his name, "Romar." Great. He was losing his mind. He needed a basketball and hoop. Or a hard run on the beach. Maybe some food. He'd had two cups of Vesta's coffee with chocolate. Coach would bench him for caffeine overload. He vaulted one of the benches to burn off some energy.

A voice whispered, "The fog comes on little cat feet."

He glanced over his shoulder. Kyra held out a plate covered with a dish towel. "That's from a poem," she said. "Here, Auntie Gram said you hadn't eaten. She made me stop right in the middle of waffles with blackberry syrup to bring you this plate. Sausage and eggs on an English muffin with toast on the side. Sheesh. She made me cut the orange, too, just in case you couldn't get it started."

"You into poetry?" he asked, reaching for the plate.

Kyra kept the plate out of reach. Her blue eyes made his heart do something that brought pain to his chest. Not the kind of pain he got running sprints or driving the key. He pushed at his glasses, though they hadn't slipped.

"Are you blind or something?" Kyra asked. "You're squinting. And I'm not into poetry, I'm into fog."

His face felt hot. "Not so blind that I can't see that breakfast sandwich getting cold."

"Sorry," she said, handing him the plate.

He took a bite, not a polite one like Granny taught him. A guy one, but he chewed with his mouth closed. That should be worth a point or two. He swallowed and asked, "So, what's with fog? Being into it?"

She shrugged. "It's like my life. I know there's something out there, I just can't see it at the moment. If I'm patient, it'll be clear."

He chewed and swallowed another bite. "That sounds like a poem." He should write down her words, use them for a poem to complete freshman English – if he got back in school.

"You must be the one into poetry," Kyra said, head tipped left, long hair falling over her shoulder and onto her arm.

He made a grunting noise like when he lifted weights. "Yeah, poetry's more or less the reason I'm here."

A bell that sounded like a school's clanged somewhere. "That's Auntie Gram's signal. I've gotta go. Catch you later."

"Yeah," he muttered, "if the authorities don't catch me first."

He poked three orange segments in his mouth, nodded to the man who'd asked for breakfast to go and carried the rest of his own out to the steps to the beach. Mingling with guests wouldn't be the best idea. The fog lifted, drifted inland and dissolved in evergreen branches. The air smelled clean. No foul camp odor. He meant to sit on a step but his thoughts pushed him down to the rocky sand and out far enough to peer around brush. Fort still there. No time to check on its occupant. Vesta needed help and he needed to close the distance between himself and the girl, Kyra, before she disappeared like the fog.

They stayed too busy for Romar to stare at her. He stole a minute to jot her words on a napkin, the ones he considered poetic, though he messed them up.

Fog hiding water and trees
my future hiding from me

Trees and me. Close enough for a rhyming poem. But the meter was wrong and the parallel didn't work, he could see that when he read it back. He could rearrange the second line. Poetry would never be his thing. He stuffed the napkin in his pants pocket and got back to cleaning the waffle iron.

Later, after they'd swept out and scrubbed up from the last of the lunch guests, Romar started the restock chores. He wheeled the hand-truck loaded with half cases of beer to the cooler, went back for soda and soft drinks, then grocery items that didn't need chilling. On one pass by the gift section, he saw a display of glass earrings like Leila wore. He backed up to read the display card.

~Healing Crystals ~
For Health, Creative Energy, Emotional Healing, Love & Fortune

Colored dots and crystal names followed in smaller print. He glanced down the list, stopping at colors that caught his eye: Amber, amethyst, emerald, garnet, jade, turquoise. Even smaller print explained the qualities of each. Ease pain, reduce anger or stress, release negativity, cleanse and balance, stimulate energy, calm fears, bring good luck or wealth, success and joy. He wondered which ones could help him stop worrying about finding his mother.

The door opened, setting off the chime like the buzzer signaling the end of half-time; get back into the game. He had work to do. While he worked, something he'd seen on the display card played with his head. He needed to read it again when things slowed down.

He needed a basketball and hoop to burn some energy. Instead, Vesta asked him to look at the lawn mower and weed eater, neither of which she'd been able to start that season. He could guess why. Both were stored in the damp garage at the RV Park end of her old building. An older Honda Civic took up most of the space. He tried to start the mower and got weak sputters. He'd tinkered with small engine equipment when his dad worked on big diesel rigs. His dad said if mowers didn't start up with a new spark plug and fresh gas, consider sending them to the dump. *Costs more to repair them than to buy new ones.*

He checked spark plugs, cleaned them, drained gas, refilled tanks from a gas can that looked reasonably new. He fiddled with the choke and tried the mower again. It started on the first tug of the starter rope. Two points. The weed eater took longer. He cleaned the spark plug with a little gas, tried again and once more. Whirrr. One point. As he mowed the lawn and trimmed brush along the fence, he thought about Kyra. He wanted to ask a couple questions about the former caretaker and drugs. Maybe they could sit on a bench by the fire after all the RV folks had gone inside for the night. He'd get her to talk about herself so he wouldn't have to say much. Maybe something witty would enter his brain and exit his mouth, and he'd get her to laugh. His arm could brush hers. He'd dig out his clean sweatshirt, have it handy on the bench in case she got cold.

"Hey," Kyra called, as he was storing the mower in the garage. "Auntie Gram and Mom think you're a godsend, they both said so. Auntie Gram was ready to buy a new mower. Anyway, I came to say goodbye. See you tomorrow morning."

"You're leaving?" he said. So much for witty.

"Gotta go," she said, her blue eyes catching a thread of light from the garage window. "The twins are with Grandma Salena who called Mom to say she's reached the end of her rope and if we don't hurry up, she'll just hang herself."

"The twins?"

"My sisters. They're eleven. Grandma caught them drinking her cooking sherry. Auntie Gram says everything's under control upstairs, take your time, get a shower or whatever." She waved and backed away.

He brushed grass clippings off his grease-stained, sweaty shirt and wondered if she could see his heart pounding through it. "Tomorrow, then," he said, meaning tomorrow he'd be clean and witty and ready to offer her a sweatshirt if it got cold.

Unless Ian Gallagher showed up and told him to pack up his gear, his uncle was on his way. Nah, that wouldn't happen. Uncle Sherman might send authorities to pick him up, but he'd never come himself.

There were a couple customers when he got back upstairs so he waited to ask Vesta if she'd heard from Ian. He wandered through the store, checking for empty spots on shelves or in the coolers. The crystal earrings gleamed in the light. He stopped to look at them again and saw what had caught his eye earlier. Words at the bottom of the card.

Crafted by Leila Jarvi.

"Leila Jarvi?" His voice boomed out like he was calling a play.

"There you are, Romar," Vesta said, and patted his arm. "You are a godsend, getting that old mower working. Leila thinks so, too."

"Her name is Jarvi? Like Granny?"

"That's her maiden name. Edmund was her father."

"Does that mean we're related or something?"

"Let's see, her daddy and your granny were cousins of some sort. Actually, Edmund and your granny's dad were first cousins. That made Edmund and Esther – your granny – first cousins once removed, so Leila would have to be twice removed and Kyra three times removed. However it works, we consider you part of the family. Fate steered you to us, and Ian's looking into legal matters."

"Legal matters?" One of Romar's hands had a firm hold on the shelf where the card of crystal earrings stood. What legal matters? He didn't want to be part of the family. Not if it made Kyra his cousin.

"Sorting out your status with your uncle and whether you're in any kind of trouble," Vesta said.

Romar struggled to swallow the saliva that collected in his mouth so he wouldn't drool like an idiot. "So, are you saying Kyra's a cousin to my granny?"

"A cousin several times removed," Vesta said, and patted his arm again. "Kissing cousins, at best. We'll sort it out tomorrow."

Romar closed his eyes and tried to get Granny to set the matter straight. He needed to know what kissing cousins meant. He liked the kissing part, but not the cousin part. Just when he meets the prettiest girl he's ever seen, and even talked with her . . . sort of talked . . . it turns out they're related somehow.

A minute later he had another thought. At least they were related on the good side, not the criminal side. Another minute ticked by before he realized he'd dissed his own mother.

9

AUNTS, UNCLES AND KISSING COUSINS

At seven the next morning Vesta said, "Sunday mornings are generally quieter than Saturdays." Leila had called to say her car wouldn't start, she didn't know when she and Kyra would be there. At seven-thirty Vesta posted a coffee-stained notice that said 'No Thermos Fills Before 10 AM'. A man from the RV Park came in with a huge thermos. The Granny voice in Romar's head described him as all spiffed up in his Sunday best, walking with a jaunty step. Maybe Granny would get around to explaining 'kissing cousins' if he paid attention.

The man read the sign, set his thermos on the floor and ordered six large coffees to go. He filled his pockets with sugar and creamer packets and stir sticks.

Vesta drilled the man with her eyes. Romar waited for him to shrivel, but he was too busy fanning a wad of bills. "You'll have to wait for the new pot," Vesta said. "We see to our seated customers first."

Coach calling the play. Romar grabbed the pot that was nearly empty, poured refills and asked at each table if he could bring them anything else.

"You could start me with one cup," Spiffy said. "I'm one of your RV guests."

"You didn't order one cup, and you could make your own coffee in your fancy rig," Vesta said. "You have a copy of my policy that explains I don't fill thermoses during breakfast rush."

"I could buy this place," Spiffy said, his eyes measuring the space.

Vesta swiped off the counter with a soapy cloth. "Make me a reasonable offer and it's yours. My personal agent will be along any time now. He's transporting the rest of my staff."

Personal agent? Staff? Romar felt his eyebrows knit, a Granny description for certain. Then the door blew open on a gust of Kyra, her mother and Ian Gallagher. Staff and personal agent right on time. Girls back at Roseburg High would roll their eyes and say "Duh" to his not getting it. Coach would have yelled "Air ball."

Confusion reigned, a full court press with tripping and fouls on both sides. Ian Gallagher saying something in code to Vesta with "Sweetheart" hanging on the end.

Leila Jarvi saying "Sorry we're so late," and adding a too long explanation about her car and a door left open with lights on until the battery died.

Kyra saying to the waiting customer, "Are you in line? For coffee? Because we're, like, desperate but we're the help so you're definitely ahead of us."

Romar, who watched her, would swear she was taunting the man. She'd edged one foot near his thermos.

"Kyra," her mother said, "watch your feet."

"I am, Mom."

Romar took a jump shot. "Score!" The word boomed, bounced off walls and came back to bite his face. "Help is here," he said, trying to get back in the game, relieved to see Vesta's auger eyes back to their usual bright lights. She even smiled at him.

Customers at all four tables watched, all silent. "Now, what can I get you folks? Hot coffee? New pot's about ready."

In the ten-thirty lull, Vesta told Romar that Ian had some information for him, and sent them to her office, one of the rooms that made up her living space behind the restaurant and store. The high Romar had been riding since Kyra arrived left him in one thud of his heart. He knew that organs didn't move around in the body like sleep walkers, but his dropped into the pit of his stomach.

Whitley would say that was more cliché than metaphor. Either way, Romar knew how it felt. Not as bad as hearing his dad died of internal injuries from his wreck. Or that Granny's nosebleed was a massive stroke. But bad enough. Sweat erupted everywhere. Even his fingernails were wet, he'd swear they were. He should have known Ian Gallagher's arrival meant more than transportation for Leila Jarvi and Kyra, last name unknown to him.

Vesta's desk was covered with neat stacks of papers weighted down by rocks that looked like they came from the beach. If any were crystals, they hid the fact inside their gray exterior. One rock nearly paper weight size settled in Romar's throat, or so it felt. Would Whitley let him use that analogy? He tried to swallow, gave up and let his voice squeak.

"The authorities are coming for me? Right?"

"Nope," Ian Gallagher said. "It's not that bad, or maybe it's worse. I spoke with your uncle and aunt. They're not amused."

"But glad to see the last of me? Now they can wash their hands of me once and for all?"

Ian scrunched his mouth so his lips disappeared. His head went down and up, down and up. "I see you're not surprised. Your aunt did mention that you left some junk – her word – in the room you used. If you want it, you'll need to make arrangements. They're not going to pack it up and ship it."

"One mostly worn out basketball and clothes that don't fit. And school books. I guess the books need to get back to the school. It's not like I had a computer or anything." Romar picked at a hangnail and noticed how white his hands looked. He'd been doing dishes without rubber gloves even though Vesta said he needed to use them. He hadn't found any that fit.

"And it seems you've left another relative without summer help. An aunt in Medford who was relying on you to learn the orchard business. Take over one day, since your aunt's husband is in poor health."

"Yeah, Aunt Arlene. Her husband's an alcoholic, so Granny said. She told me to give them a wide berth. You know what that means?"

Ian narrowed his eyes. "Yes, I do. Your uncle Sherman made it sound like you squandered your chance at an inheritance."

Romar shook his head. "They don't own the orchard, they just manage it. I only met Aunt Arlene one time, at Granny's funeral. She asked Uncle Sherman for money. For her fair share of Granny's money when the estate was settled. Or if she could borrow something in the meantime. Stuff like that."

"And what did your uncle say to that?"

"Same thing he said when Granny or I asked about my dad's estate. Medical expenses and funeral expenses ate up most of the money. He and Aunt Joan were covering extras for Granny and me."

"Did your granny have money of her own?"

He shrugged. "Her social security. But she said there should be money from the sale of the Glide house. She helped Dad when he first bought it. She used money from my grandpa's pension. That was before I was born. Granny thought there should be something left, even after Uncle Sherman and Aunt Joan paid themselves back."

"Did you ever see any legal papers? House sale documents? Bank statements?"

"They figured I was too young for that. They kept saying, 'What money there was went into a trust fund for Romar. We're taking care of you both. Don't worry.'" He paused while Ian frowned, then continued.

"I asked for money from the fund for decent glasses, but they said no, it was set up to be untouched until I went to college. Granny paid for my Rec Specs and extra food. I mean, I ate a lot, but it's not like I'm fat or anything. Uncle Sherman and Aunt Joan covered all my regular expenses, but Granny paid for special stuff like Gatorade and breakfast cereal I liked. Aunt Joan told me at least once a week that they provided 'Relative foster care, without any case worker snooping around, thank you very much.' She said it was the decent thing to do."

Ian Gallagher ran a hand over his face. Romar looked at Ian's fingers, long and slender, good for picking up the little screws used in glasses frames.

"Did you ever see anything with the word *trust* on it? Or any other papers concerning you?"

"I saw the paper that said they were my legal guardians and some medical records that said I was fit to play sports."

"That's one of the major issues you need to consider. Health care insurance. Before we get into that, let me ask this. Now that you've been away from your uncle and aunt for a week or so, would you consider going back until you finish high school?"

Romar shook his head, swallowed so hard it hurt his chest and forced out a whispered "No. I can't live with them without Granny. And I need to find my mother. I need to know what she looks like."

"Okay. Okay." Ian unfolded a piece of paper. "The Internet's a great tool, by the way. I learned you're old enough to qualify for a program the state calls Independent Living. We can look into that and some other possibilities. But, first, you need to call your uncle and aunt yourself. Vesta said to use her phone."

The time had come. He'd known it would. A chill ran down his body. His stomach did the flips, but his hand remained steady. When his uncle barked, "Hello," he said, "Hello, Uncle Sherman," and held the phone away from his head. The conversation started like he'd expected.

"So, you decided to run off, just like your mother, no thought to how that affects others. You'll end up in jail, just like her."

His uncle's snarling voice made Romar determined to keep his own normal. "No, I won't end up in jail. You've been telling me since Granny and I moved in with you that it's time for me to earn my own way."

"Just walk out the door and leave your shit behind for someone else to clean up. Leave your aunt Arlene without summer help."

Romar took in a deep breath. He wouldn't shout back in his own defense and let his uncle win the round. In the background he could hear his aunt going on about his school books. He let out the breath and swallowed.

"I'll find someone from school to pick up my books. The rest can go to Goodwill or into the garbage."

"Garbage collection costs money. Irresponsibility costs a whole helluva lot more, did you ever think about that? Did you ever think about what it cost Joan and me, not just money but time and aggravation, to provide a home for you and your grandmother?"

"You made it clear to me every day. Money and aggravation, that's all you ever talked about to me. You never even asked me about school, or a basketball game." One rebel tear found its way onto his face. He wouldn't cry; he wouldn't let Uncle Sherman hear him losing it.

His voice turned harsh, unfamiliar. "You act like you know everything about life, but you never figured out the most important thing. Granny was your mother. She loved you. She saw to you."

Ian touched his knee with one hand and took the phone from him with the other.

"Ian Gallagher here, Mr. Jones. I'm speaking on Romar's behalf. There are some logistics to discuss, some legal issues. As I told you yesterday, the widow of your mother's cousin, Edmund Jarvi, lives in Yachats. That makes you related. Romar is currently working for Mrs. Jarvi's sister, Vesta Palmateer."

Ian paused for a long moment of head nodding. "Yes, they're aware of Romar's circumstances."

Romar needed to blow his nose, but his uncle would hear. He grabbed a tissue and held it like he had a nosebleed.

Ian scribbled on the back of the list he'd pulled from his pocket. "I understand," he said. "My attorney will contact you to iron that out. Romar's situation permits him to select an independent living status that legally clears you and your wife of all responsibility. He can complete his freshman credits online through your school district."

Romar's heart shot back into its proper place behind his rib cage, still pounding but for a different reason. He could finish his school year. Granny wouldn't have to be disappointed in him. He swallowed the quart of saliva that had puddled in his mouth.

When Ian hung up the phone, Romar said, "Is that true? That I can complete my credits online?"

"It's true."

"Well, then, I'll need to get to a library. To use a computer. Which means I'll need to work out a schedule with Vesta for when I can be gone."

"Whoa," Ian said, frown wrinkling his forehead. "I didn't expect quite so much enthusiasm from a guy who walked out of school two weeks before the end of the year. How were you doing with grades before you left?"

"Acing math and science. Doing okay in freshman English, except for poetry, that's the unit Whitley had us on when he told me to take a hike. Doing okay in social studies."

Ian frowned. "A teacher *told* you to take a hike?"

"He gave me a choice. Pay attention or take a hike. It was hard to pay attention after Granny died, especially in English that's . . . you know . . . sort of a slow subject, especially if other kids are reading. So, I'd just go off in a basketball game in my head. Mr. Whitley sort of gave me a chance to make a decision, so I took my books and headed for the principal's office. That's what 'Take a hike' means. Report to the principal."

"Ah. And your grades are okay to good?"

"Yep."

"And you play basketball?"

"Freshman ball. You have to be a sophomore to go out for varsity."

"Were you a regular?"

"Starting center. But I can play any position, it's just because I'm tall that coach made me center. Same position in junior high. Same reason."

"How did your uncle feel about that?"

Romar shrugged, bony shoulders almost touching his earlobes. "He and Aunt Joan weren't really into basketball."

"What were they into?"

"Pub darts. They were on a team."

"Christ Almighty," Ian said.

More coffee dripped into the restaurant's pots. Vesta was elbow deep in pasta salad, the sight of which set off Romar's stomach. "Will you men check the cooler stock?" Vesta called. "Leila's running short on fruit drinks. And set up the shelter for a picnic. We'll be serving down there at 12:30. Blame Kyra. She said we could handle it. A family reunion of some sort."

Kyra, busy making deli sandwiches, looked their way, shrugged and smiled. Romar had never gotten a smile like that from a girl at

Roseburg High. He smiled back and winked. Far as he could remember, he'd never winked on purpose in his entire life. Blinked plenty of times trying to see something. Or to get a lash out of his eye.

Granny said his long dark lashes would be the envy of every girl he met, once he took off his glasses and let them be seen. The problem with that, with his glasses off he couldn't see if a girl looked envious, or looked at all.

He checked with Leila before heading for the back cooler. She named specific brands and flavors, then said, "What's your sun sign, Romar?"

"Huh?" he said, his brain still processing the phone call, Kyra's smile, and bottled drinks he'd never tried.

"Your birth date?"

"January 25th."

"Aha. Aquarius. Impulsive. But intelligent and analytical. It so fits."

"Fits what?"

"You. Vesta said you just up and walked out of school one morning, and headed this way because your granny grew up here, though you'd never been here before. I'd call that impulsive."

"I guess. Yeah, okay, whatever."

When he returned, Leila held out her closed hand. "Here, put this in your pocket. It's aventurine."

"Adventuring?"

Leila laughed. "It does sound like that, it was found by accident. This one's a green quartz with bits of hematite. See, the bits catch the light. They'll help with all sorts of things. Muscle cramps in your legs, for one. The aventurine will heal your heart."

"Oh, a healing crystal." How did she know he got muscle cramps in his legs? Granny called them growing pains when he got them in the middle of the night.

"Yes, and do not make fun, do not laugh at the notion. It doesn't matter if you believe in the healing power of crystals . . . yet. This will help. Keep it in your pocket where you can touch it. When you go to bed, lie down on your back and place it on your chest. Trust me, it will do wonders. I'll put together some other crystals for you. This is just a starter. I had it in mind even before I knew for sure you were an Aquarian."

Romar imagined the crystal performing some magic while he packed food and drinks down to the shelter. Mist collected on the plastic wrap, not enough to make a rain drop sound, just enough for Kyra to worry the sandwiches would get wet. She played point guard, directing the set-up. Tables and benches circled the fire pit. Food stretched out buffet style in two lines.

He got a fire going and followed her game plan. He counted six women, five men and eleven children in the group that lined up with plates. One man and woman seemed to be grandparents to all the kids. They heaped whipped topping on strawberry Jell-o and promised they'd make S'mores later.

The food went fast. Kyra got bossy a couple of times.

"Rearrange the sandwiches so the trays don't look so empty or lopsided."

He frowned at that one until he saw the difference when she moved remaining sandwiches to the middle of the trays.

"Put all the pasta salad into one bowl, and get the empty bowl out of here. And bring down some more Jell-o and chips for the kids."

"Yes, coach." He leaned down and kissed her cheek.

"Knock it off," she said. "We're working."

"I'm impulsive," he said. "Your mother says so. She gave me a crystal. Green aventurine."

She dumped utensils into the empty bowl he held. "Crystals are supposed to cure problems, not cause them." And then she grinned.

He carried off the bowl and utensils, a smile on his face. Finally a *good* problem, one he hoped he could handle.

10

FAMILY MATTERS

Romar banked coals in the shelter fire pit to keep them ready for the group to roast marshmallows for S'mores. He and Kyra had packed the last of the mess to the kitchen and put tables and benches back in order. The kids, full of Jell-o and chips, were all over the place, in and out of rigs that had pulled in Friday afternoon while he was on the beach sniffing out the driftwood and tarp camp. He hadn't helped any of them with hook-ups.

"Notice anything special about that group?" Kyra asked.

"Yeah, one of the girls was really cute." He grinned, thinking Kyra was really cute.

Kyra rolled her eyes. "Anything about the adults?"

"Let's see, one was a Grandpa and one was a Grandma. I know that for a fact because the little kids called them that."

Kyra stared at him like Whitley did when he waited for an answer about the meaning of a poem. Bzzt. Foul on him.

"We're talking about the other adults . . . not the grandparents, right?"

She nodded, hands on her hips.

"That's easy, there were five women and four men besides the grandparents. Three of the women looked really good for moms. One looked okay except for gray hair and mustard drips down her sweat shirt. And glaring at you."

"Glaring at me?"

"Right. She asked, 'Who made these sandwiches?' and I pointed at you."

Kyra frowned. He wasn't getting it. He tried again.

"Plus there was the one with frizzy hair who seemed mad about something. She scowled a lot and slammed things around."

Kyra's hands stayed on her hips. He'd hit the rim but missed the shot.

"What?" he asked.

"The men. There were men. One Grandpa and four Dads."

"Yeah, I got that, I'm pretty good in math."

Kyra's eyebrows shot up. "How good? Like, in algebra?"

"Grade-wise?" He shrugged. "I was acing it 'til I walked out."

"All right. Stick around, help me get through algebra . . . I have to make up for dropping it . . . and I'll fix you up with every crystal ever identified."

He squinted out of habit, but it didn't help. "Nice move," he said, hands and feet pantomiming a dribble dance.

"I already guessed you're into basketball, and I'm not dodging anything. I'm serious. Vesta wants you to stay here, and so do Grandma Salena and my mom. Because you're a man. Don't you get it?"

He shrugged again and held out his hands, palms up, no more dribbling. "Nope."

She went "Ohhhh," like she'd collapse under the weight of whatever he didn't get. She did something with her eyes that put him on guard.

"Their family reunion had men. And boy children. See, when our family gets together we only have a man if we borrow Ian Gallagher, and he's not related to any of us. We're trying to change that. He'd marry Auntie Gram Vesta in a nanosecond if she'd sell this business and move to Waldport."

"Waldport?"

"Right, Waldport, I'll get to that in a minute. Once you understand the man thing. There aren't any in our family. Or, to be accurate, there haven't been until you came along."

"Uh . . ."

"Just listen, so you get it. There's Vesta and her daughter Coral and Coral's daughter who's a snob. Her name doesn't matter. They live in Eugene where Coral works for the university. Are you keeping track?"

"Three," he said. "I could count that far when I was two."

"Okay, then there's Grandma Salena. We call her Salty. She had one son, he's dead, his wife remarried and we never see her and their two kids who happen to be girls anyway, so, who needs them? That makes my mom's Salty's only living child.

"My mom had me by a guy who left before I was born. Far as I know, he doesn't exist, he didn't even leave his name. Jarvi's the name on my birth certificate. We had a man around for awhile, long enough to let me call him Daddy and to give us my twin sisters. Until he went off crab fishing in Alaska, one of the world's most dangerous jobs. He's 'lost at sea,' which makes it tough to get child support out of him.

"If you kept count, that's eight females, not counting the ones by my dead uncle that we never see, without a living male relative. Except you."

"Me?"

Kyra didn't slow down long enough to nod. "The way Vesta and Salty figure, you're related because Salty was married to Edmund Jarvi who was a cousin to your grandmother. They've been talking about you coming out here to live ever since Salty got a letter from your grandma last Christmas telling them to keep an eye out for you."

That's when Romar sat down. Or, to be honest, fell onto a bench that happened to be close enough to keep him from landing tailbone first on the cement. "Last Christmas?"

Kyra sat beside him. "Around then. She had a stroke around then, right?"

He blinked and looked away. He didn't want to remember that time, that first stroke when his aunt started a full court press for a nursing home and his uncle took it under consideration.

Kyra leaned across his arm and kissed his cheek. "That's for being a guy who loved his grandma. And payback for the one you snuck in on my cheek earlier."

"Next time I'm aiming for the lips," he said. That surprised him, coming out of his mouth.

"Okay, lips next time," she said. "If you stick around."

"Yeah, well, I'll be around long enough to save up some money to get to Washington."

"Where your mother's in prison. I know about that."

Romar glanced sideways at Kyra, who stayed right beside him on the bench, like talking about a mother in prison was no big deal. Every teacher he'd had in grade school, and then counselors at junior high, told him not to tell other kids. Teachers at Roseburg High didn't seem to know, but one counselor did. One weird counselor. Kids found out on their own, somehow.

"Yeah, you all . . . you and your mom and Vesta and Ian Gallagher know a lot. Do you know how to get me inside the prison?"

He didn't do sarcasm well, especially when he had to keep emotion out of his voice. He got to his feet, grabbed the fire poker, stirred the coals.

"My grandma and Auntie Gram are all over that like you'd be all over a basketball if one fell from the rafters right now. They figure if one of them gets on your mother's approved visitor list, you can get inside, too."

He spun around to look at her. "Whoa, back up. Why would they even want to get on her list? Why would they want to go inside a prison when they don't have to?"

Kyra stood then, and put her hands back on her hips. "You haven't been paying attention. They want you to be part of our family. Like, forever."

"Yeah, paying attention's been a problem for me." Only since his granny died, but he didn't say that. He liked it at Vesta's, but forever was a little too much to think about when he hadn't found his mother.

"Okay. I'll run it by you again. Your grandmother and my grandfather were sort of cousins. Grandpa died when I was eight. I still miss him every day. He paid attention to me when everyone else was busy with the twins."

Romar nodded. He'd gotten their grandparents' connection, and he understood the attention part, too.

"So, see, Grandpa died, and then the twins' dad went away and never came back, and then Uncle Gramp, Auntie Gram's husband, died. He'd been sick, but still we had him around."

"I'm sorry." He knew how lame that sounded; he'd heard it often enough. Maybe he should put his arms around her, pat her on the back or something, but she didn't exactly give him a chance.

"So, here's the deal, if you want it. You stay here, help me get through make-up algebra this summer, keep working for Auntie Gram Vesta, unless she's smart enough to sell this place and move to Waldport to live with Ian Gallagher. We all worry about her out here. Ian gave her an air horn for a Christmas present. She's supposed to sound it if there's ever a burglar."

"An air horn. To stop a burglar." He pictured the guy he'd seen in the dunes. Someone crazy enough to break in, maybe wave a gun. "An air horn. Wow! That should scare a burglar. He'd drop his gun and run."

"Well she's supposed to dial nine one one, too. And call Ian, but he's clear up in Waldport. Speaking of which, that's where you should go to school. The basketball team could use some new talent."

"That would require me getting into school."

"You will. Ian's already on that."

"I'd still have to make the basketball team."

"You will. I'll talk to the coach tomorrow. He'll be stoked."

He shook his head. "That's not how it works. I earn a spot or I don't, that's on me."

"Well, it can't hurt to have a family connection."

He made the time-out signal. "I'm not thrilled about being related to you. I mean, I like you, so it sort of gets in the way of . . . you know. Going out, and stuff like that."

Kyra wrinkled her nose. "We're not exactly close enough, as relatives go, to produce a village idiot, you know. Not that we'd ever produce anything since I'm not planning to have kids. Besides, I'm not exactly into going out, and I'm really not into . . . stuff."

"What are you into?"

"Drama. Right now, I want to write and direct a play. Someday, I'll make documentary films."

Romar grinned. "Yeah, that fits you. You're very dramatic."

"I learned it from Grandma Salty. When school starts, you and I can act like we're an item. That'll take care of some other things."

"An item?"

"You know, like we hang together."

He pushed up his glasses and shook his head. "No, no acting. We could be an item or not, but not an act. I'm not into drama."

Kyra moved her hands from her hips to the back pockets of her jeans. She tilted her head to one side and then the other. "Okay," she said. "If I pass algebra."

"What other things?"

"Huh?"

"You said acting like an item will take care of some other things."

"Like guys hanging around where they're not wanted."

"So, I'd be on defense? Blocking out guys so you could make it through the halls to your classes."

"Something like that."

"But first, before I do anything about school anywhere, I need to find my mother. There are some things I need to know. Could be I'll want to live in Washington. You know, be close enough to visit."

"You'll find her. That part's covered, and I'm going along for the trip when Salty takes you. I've never been out of Oregon."

"Me neither. Could be I'll like Washington better."

Kyra tilted her head. "No. You'd miss us. Especially Vesta. Besides, once you finish helping me with algebra, you can help me write a play about visiting inside a women's prison."

Waves crashed on the beach. They must have been crashing all along, but he hadn't noticed. A bird flew into the shelter and settled on a table. Kyra stood on her tiptoes and kissed him on the lips. A quick kiss he tried to hang onto, but she wiggled away. Blood pounded in his head.

"We'll be a good non-acting act," she said.

11

SETTLED IN BY THE SEA

Vesta's bell clanged, calling them back to work. Kyra took off up the incline. Romar followed, hoping she'd slip on the wet grass so he could help her. Be the man. That should rank right up there with getting the lawn mower and weed eater working.

Not that he was all that sure about being the man. Or having Kyra's grandma Salena take him to visit his mother in prison. He needed time to set up his own game plan, think about what Granny would say. Kyra made it sound like Granny sent him to this family of women, but that didn't mean his granny wanted them to run his life.

He definitely didn't want Kyra to say anything about him to the basketball coach. He needed to make that clear. Soon as the three women inside gave him a chance to speak.

He was pretty sure Granny would want him to stand up for himself.

Before the door had swung all the way open, Leila said, "Hurry up, Kyra, we've got to get home. Salty's reached her limit with the twins."

"Romar, two rigs are ready to pull out," Vesta said. "Eleven and seventeen."

"So, who hasn't reached their limits with those two?" Kyra said. "They're out of control."

"Hush a minute," Vesta said. "I need to send Romar out to check the disconnects . . . the water valves and sewer hookups. Electricity, too, but most of them remember that much. Just make sure everything's capped off tight as can be."

"Eleven and seventeen," he said.

Leila and Kyra kept the tiff over the twins going, something about the girls being Kyra's sisters and Leila's daughters. Vesta gave up on hushing them and raised her voice.

"Do you know what I mean? Check their disconnects? It seems like someone should take time to show you how to do things, but I'm about to be abandoned by those two, and Ian's already off and gone."

"I'm all over it, Coach. Eleven's the guy who wanted the thermos of coffee and Seventeen's the one who had so much trouble backing his rig in."

Vesta's forehead wrinkled. "Now, how did you remember that?"

"I helped them hook up. They weren't part of the caravan that came in while I was on the beach."

Kyra stopped right in the middle of her argument with her mom to say, "He's some kind of mathematical genius, he's going to help me get through algebra."

"Time out," Romar said. "The rigs are like opponents in a basketball game, not a math problem. In basketball, you make mental notes of who's where and how they move. Some you pay more attention to than others. Eleven wore clothes that didn't look right for the beach and Seventeen needs new glasses."

"Kyra," Leila said, "we're leaving. Now. Bye, Romar. I'll be back in a couple days with an assortment of crystals for you to use when you meditate."

"Right, crystals," Romar said, his eyes on Kyra who stood behind her mother doing some exasperated girl thing with her eyes and mouth. "Gotta go. Eleven and Seventeen are waiting."

Most of the rigs pulled out before sunset. Romar scraped a chunk of skin off one knuckle getting a connection loosened on a motor home. He wiped the blood on his pants, saying "Sorry, Granny."

Vesta fussed over him, cleaning and bandaging the spot. Then she fed him assorted leftovers from lunch and chocolate chip cookies right out of the oven from dough she bought ready to bake. It reminded him how much he missed his granny, and that he needed to find his mother before he got too comfortable at Vesta's by the Sea.

"You need some beach time, Romie. Time to chase the waves. Things should be quiet for a couple days. Monday, at least. You've been going non-stop since you got here."

He nodded. Chocolate chip cookies warm from the oven and cold milk were too good to take time out to answer.

"That should take care of things," Vesta said. "Your helping Kyra with algebra, I mean. She's a smart girl; she wants to go to college. We put most of what she earns here into a college fund, some into a driver's license fund. She'll be sixteen in September, so she'll need to pay for driver's education. Car insurance, too."

"Uh, about the algebra thing, that's not for sure. And other things Kyra said . . . well, being around her is sort of like stepping into quicksand." Like he'd done back in the dunes, but he knew mentioning that would lead the conversation off in another direction.

"Oh, dear." Vesta made a sound like air going out of a punctured basketball. "Kyra tends to get ahead of herself. What did she say this time?"

"Uh, something about her grandmother getting on my mother's prison visiting list so she can help me get inside."

Vesta shook her head. "That's all Kyra thinking out loud. She comes up with ideas, bandies them about and makes them into facts while the rest of us are trying to catch up."

"So, it's not like all of you planned . . . things . . . together."

"No, not really. Salena and I may have talked about an idea or two. She's my older sister. I run things by her. She might have said something to Leila in Kyra's hearing. All told, we're an odd lot, like survivors that washed up on the beach in a leaky raft. We're always planning ahead to avert the next crisis."

Romar thought she looked tired. The lights in her eyes seemed dull. She patted his hand, the one with the scraped knuckle. It smarted, but he didn't mind. "Like Kyra's planning on me attending Waldport High."

"We'll see to school, if you choose to stay here with me," Vesta said. "We sort of hoped your grandmother told you about us. When you showed up, I thought she might have sent you. Until you said you stopped in here by chance. Salena said your grandmother worried about you staying on with your uncle and aunt. So, you see, we've been planning your life since last Christmas." She took in a deep breath that lifted her shoulders. When she breathed out, they dropped. "We haven't been fair to you."

"That's not true. You've been more fair than . . . than a runaway should expect." He almost said they'd been more fair than his uncle and aunt, but that wasn't really true. His uncle and aunt did provide for Granny and him.

"I don't think of you as a runaway. It's more like you're the breath of fresh air I needed. Still, this isn't much of a life for a teenager, being stuck out here, five or six miles from Yachats, another eight to Waldport, if that's where you decide to go to school."

"Maybe I should just stay out of school for a year. Work here long as you need me. Save some money for health insurance and clothes. Get to where I can pay my way."

"I suspect your granny would say you need to get back into school. And Ian says you need a basketball court to work out on. The only decent one around here, according to him, is at Waldport High. Ian would be happy to have you live with him during the school week. His place is right in Waldport, but I'm hoping to figure out a way to keep you here."

"Keep me here because you knew my granny? Who was related to your sister Salena's husband? And you don't have any male relatives around?" It didn't seem like a good enough reason.

"No, Romie, because I knew the minute the door closed behind you last Wednesday evening that you were sent here by some unknown force in the universe to fill an empty spot in my heart. And now, before I start blubbering, I'm going to wrap some cookies for you to take downstairs. Take milk and water and whatever drinks you'd like."

He went, glad to be alone inside the caretaker's room. He started doing stretches, then sit-ups and push-ups. Coach always said, "Keep your head in the game." When he walked into Vesta's by the Sea five nights ago, he'd stepped into a game he didn't understand.

He liked it, though. More or less.

Before sunup the next morning, he dressed for a run, did some stretches and headed for packed sand near the water's edge, scanning the distance to the south. No blue tarp. Waves built and broke near his feet. Halfway to the headland, he tugged off his sweatshirt and looped it around his neck.

On the way back, he ran in soft sand, going for the burn. The camper had left charred wood, rocks split in the fire, scattered garbage that attracted critters. He wondered if it had been the same guy he'd seen that morning in the dunes. Could be he made that up out of his imagination, then embellished it with bits and pieces he picked up from Kyra's comments about the former caretaker, and from little things the adults did. Ian's silent message to Vesta; Leila's and Vesta's warnings to Kyra; their looks ping-ponging their secret thoughts.

Embellished. A Whitley word. Romar would be glad when he finished freshman English so he could quit feeling guilty about walking out of the man's classroom.

Wednesday afternoon, when Vesta told him to take the rest of the day off, he walked along Highway 101 to a spot with access to the national forest. He followed a creek inland, hiked beyond a stand of maple and alder to dense evergreens. When he didn't spot a trail, he stayed close to the creek. The sound of moving water, not crashing waves, took him back to Glide, to the house where he grew up. This creek was quiet compared to the river, but it would do. The forest grew dense and dark within minutes. He found a spot two or three yards from the creek where he could sit on dry needles and breathe in the smell of Douglas fir. Western hemlock, too. The evergreens' fragrance helped him think about all that had happened since he'd walked into Vesta's a week ago. There were some things he needed to sort out about his own family, especially his dad.

This is what he knew. Roland Jones dropped out of college after two years, giving up his plans to get a forestry degree. He became a licensed river and backwoods guide for the Umpqua River and National Forest. In the off-season, he worked on riverboat repairs and diesel trucks.

This is what he was still sorting out. Roland died a few months before his thirty-fourth birthday, when Romar was thirteen. That meant Roland became a father at age twenty. He'd dropped out of college to support his family, but his wife left him soon after their baby was born. Roland's mother raised the baby. They became the family: Roland, his mother Esther, and his infant son Romar.

He'd tried to put it all together before, with Granny's help, but it seemed like he didn't know what questions to ask. Granny always tried to reassure him that it wasn't his fault. *Your mother was awfully young when you were born. Only seventeen.* He wondered why his granny never mentioned that his dad was young, too. Only twenty, with a new baby.

The fresh pungent forest called up memories of hikes he'd taken with his dad. Hikes where they talked about saving for college so Romar could get a degree that would prepare him to help manage and save the national forests. That dream started eroding when he and Granny moved out of Glide to live with Uncle Sherman and Aunt Joan. They'd made it clear they wouldn't help him with college. Aunt Joan wanted him gone when he turned eighteen. Uncle Sherman said he could stay until graduation, an extra five months, if he behaved.

Their idea of sending him to Aunt Arlene didn't surface until after Granny died. He'd always behaved until then, until the day he walked out of school, gathered up his clothes and his dad's pack and set out to find his mother. Now, working out some truths, he wondered what good finding her would do. Free him from wondering why she left him, he guessed. Answer his questions about what he'd done that was so bad she'd decided to walk out of his life.

12

GOING ONLINE

After spending an hour or so sorting those memories and thoughts, Romar started back, stepping carefully to avoid damaging plants growing in the understory. His dad's pack had a couple well-worn books about identifying plants. He'd carry it along the next time he crossed the highway. He'd learn plant identification to honor his dad.

By the time he got back to Vesta's by the Sea he thought of Highway 101 as a dividing line between his old life with his dad and Granny, and his new life with Vesta and her family.

The east side of the highway represented forests with trees that seemed like old friends, smells that carried him back to Glide and hikes with his dad.

The west side represented the ocean that Granny loved and lived without because she tended to him. Staying close to the ocean, to Yachats, seemed like the right thing to do for Granny. He wanted to believe that she knew where he was, and could see that he liked the ocean, too.

Things stayed quiet the rest of that day until he told Vesta about his walk in the woods. They were finishing dinner together, soup and sandwiches like she'd given him the night he first met her.

"That's a national wilderness area over there," she said, arms waving. "It's part of the Siuslaw National Forest, but it's more wild. You could get lost in there."

The worried look on her face reminded him of Granny when he'd been late getting home, or when he wandered too close to the river when they lived in Glide.

"I followed a creek. I didn't go far. I'm sort of okay about hiking alone in the woods. My dad took me out a lot. But, you know, a hiker's guide is important, and I don't have one, which is why I kept the creek in sight."

"I have hikers' guides in my office. Terrain maps. Or are they called topographic maps? A file drawer full of them for my guests to borrow, but most of them don't come here to hike in the forest. Hikers usually camp at the public campgrounds."

Vesta's arms kept waving while she talked. She led him into her office, loaded him down with books and file folders, and told him her office was his to use any time he wanted.

"Take what you want downstairs, then come right back up. You can tell me more about your hike over a piece of cheesecake I didn't sell today. I want to hear about your dad. I know a bit about your granny, but not about him."

She locked the door when he came back inside so she could listen without being interrupted. His dad's story made her cry a little, even before the part about the wreck on an icy road, and the big buck that he must have tried to avoid hitting.

He avoided the damp eye bit, but he used up a couple napkins blowing his nose.

The next day, Ian Gallagher brought him a used laptop and hooked it up to the Internet, complete with an email address. Excited as Romar was, things got a little tense when he asked Ian for a bill and payment plan. Ian frowned and did some odd things with his mouth.

"Is this your granny's influence? This asking for a bill?"

They were in Romar's room, sitting at the table with a view across the narrow stretch of grass and a row of shrubs to the Pacific Ocean. He watched the waves while he looked for a nice way to say he was afraid of strings that might be attached. Ian and Vesta were both giving him too much. Kyra was expecting too much.

"Yeah, pretty much Granny, but my dad, too. They taught me about responsibility. I need to pay my own way in life now, with them both gone. Granny knew I didn't much like it at Uncle Sherman and Aunt Joan's, but she said they were still family."

He shrugged, meaning to end the conversation, but his mouth didn't get the message. "I should have left there when she died. I should have told them I'd never go to Aunt Arlene's for the summer, that I needed to find my mother even if they thought it was a bad idea, that I didn't like depending on them for a roof over my head, and that I didn't plan to ever work in the mill like Uncle Sherman. But, I didn't, and now I'm here where it's nice. Big-time nice. There's a lot I have to figure out, not just how to pay my way. Other stuff, like who I am."

Ian took off his glasses to rub his eyes. "It's a used computer, Romar. There are no resale shops around here. In fact, most places would charge me to take it off my hands, and they'd send it out to recycle."

Romar stood, flexed his back and shoulders, did some squats. "Yeah, it's used, but the Internet and e-mail hook-up cost."

Ian sighed. "Look, I'll prepare a bill. Vesta wants to help you, and I do too. We don't want to take over your life." After a moment he added, "I wish I'd met your granny and dad."

"Excuse me," Romar said. He needed to live up to the examples his dad and Granny set for him. He went into the bathroom, took off his glasses, splashed cold water on his face and put on a smile that he hoped looked appreciative. He needed to keep his head in the game. Keep his emotions under control, not let them control him. It all made his head pound.

Ian had Waldport High School up on the computer screen when Romar came back out. Together, they went through information the site provided. The school had 242 students in grades nine through twelve. They offered all the standard courses plus some vocational choices. Playing basketball, or any other sport, would cost one hundred dollars.

"I'll fill you in on some other info not listed on this site," Ian said. "The school district has a program they call School Matters. It helps with school fees . . . provides free lunch . . . offers tutoring. It doesn't sound like you'll need tutoring, but what about the fees or lunch?"

Romar shook his head. "I'd rather work full time and do all my schooling online."

After a moment, Ian said "I don't think you'll need to do that. You may need to appear in court though, with an attorney, to request emancipation under the law. That way you're legally on your own. Your uncle and aunt can continue to serve as trustees for the remainder of your dad's estate, or you can petition for someone else to take it over. There may not be much money. I think we can ask them to give you an accurate accounting. I suspect any trustee would decide it needs to be saved until you enroll in college."

Romar nodded. Sadness had a grip on him. "Okay. That's okay, saving it for college. Thanks for all the help." The headache was getting worse.

"And, you might want to look into the high school in Florence. It's bigger by three times or so."

"Nah, I'd rather try Waldport. At least I'd know one person."

"You'll need an address in the district. Did Vesta explain that?"

"Sort of." Romar stared at the computer screen like it might tell him what to say next. No help there. "Can I ask you something? About that?"

"Of course you may."

Ian didn't smile or touch him or act like a priest or anything. Not that Romar knew how priests acted except from TV. He just waited. But he didn't cross his arms, either, like Uncle Sherman did when he said he would listen.

"It's about something Kyra said. About their family being all females, and I'm sort of related to her grandfather, and they'd like me to be part of the family."

"Uh huh," Ian said. "Kyra tends to dwell on the all-female thing."

Romar rubbed the bandaged knuckle, needing the smarting pain to help him say what bothered him. "Yeah, well, I have a mother. I guess that means I'm part of her family. If she has any. I need to figure out what to do about being her son. I don't think I'm ready to be part of another family."

Ian nodded. "That makes sense to me." He pushed the computer aside so it wasn't front and center anymore. "Did you tell Vesta what Kyra said?"

"Some of it. The part about her grandma would get on my mother's visiting list and take me to the prison to visit. But not that Kyra wants to go along."

"That could be difficult to manage, given Leila's work schedule and the need for someone to care for the twins."

"Oh," Romar said, relieved. "I really like Kyra. She's pretty, and she's fun to talk to, it's just that I don't have a clue when it comes to girls. I never know what to say."

He'd been interested in a girl at the beginning of ninth grade, one who acted nice to him. They lasted about two weeks. She lost interest in him once basketball practice began in early November. She wanted a guy to take her places after school, one with money to spend. She didn't want a guy worrying about his granny's health.

"None of us has a clue when it comes to girls," Ian said.

Romar smiled at that. "Besides which, I guess I'm pretty messed up, according to my school counselor. After Granny died, she talked to me about grief work and some stress scale. I had a copy of it. She gave me points for the bad things that happened." He counted them off on his fingers like a little kid practicing addition.

"My dad being killed, Granny dying, moving from Glide, changing schools, my mother abandoning me."

"I've seen that stress scale," Ian said. "It's designed to put things in perspective."

"Yeah, but she lost the perspective when she heard about the prison thing. She really latched onto that, asking me how that made me feel. She gave me a list of words so I could choose a feeling. I said pretty much all of them."

Ian nodded like he understood the stress scale and the feelings thing, too.

"Then she added in points for the good stuff, like playing basketball. She said good stress rated too. I had the highest total number she'd ever seen for a kid my age. I think she got off on that, know what I mean? Like, she had a real case to work on."

"Yes," Ian said, "I do know. In the end, I think we all find our own way. Not that counselors don't help. Some do, sometimes. I've been working on the grief thing since my wife died. Five years, now. My friendship with Vesta and her family helps."

"Yeah, Vesta reminds me of my granny. It's going to be hard to leave her and this place, but I have to go. One of these days, not right away. I walked away from Roseburg with two goals – getting some of Granny's ashes to Smelt Sands Beach, and finding my mother. I have to take care of that second goal."

"I understand. Just let Vesta know before you take off."

13

THE WILDERNESS

Friday afternoon Vesta said, "Take a break. Take that walk in the woods like you've been wanting to do. I've got you working too many hours. If anyone saw your time sheet, I'd be in serious trouble."

"Yeah, and if anyone saw how much I eat they'd tell you to get rid of me." Romar didn't keep track of hours on and hours off. Since he lived on the premises, it seemed like he should be available whenever needed. They'd been busy all day with RV hookups and what Vesta called walk-ins grabbing food to take to the beach.

He checked stock in the grocery section, wandered through the parked rigs and shelter, making sure all was in order. Then he crossed the highway, cut through a stand of scrub growth to an old wagon trail he'd read about in one of Vesta's hiker guides. There were good views of the ocean and Vesta's place from the trail. If he had his dad's camera, he could take some pictures for her.

Aunt Joan told him they'd never found the camera after the accident. She suspected the wrecker truck driver took it. Romar suspected Aunt Joan took it herself and sold it along with other things he would have liked to keep.

He shook his head to get rid of that thought. It didn't change anything. He climbed higher along a trodden area, enjoying the challenge, the familiar forest scent, the tightening in his calves. He followed a path, narrower than a trail, that suggested animals or other hikers had cut through. It ended in a cleared plateau. Fir and hemlock branches filtered the ocean view and Vesta's, and blocked the sound of waves breaking on the beach. From the elevation where he stood, the structures and buildings looked flat. He gauged the spot at six hundred feet above sea level, give or take.

He explored the clearing's perimeter, puzzled by its shape. Like a hiking boot with a thick heel. The boot's toe sloped down to broken fir branches. A wind gust must have ripped across the clearing, he figured, until he got a look at the branches' trunk ends. They hadn't snapped off. Someone had sawed and hacked them with dull tools, and stacked them with purpose. Like a blind. Could be a hunter waiting for deer or elk to wander into the clearing.

He picked up a sturdy limb, needles still green and pliable, and poked at the pile. A stench like one he and his dad had once encountered rose and burned his nostrils. He backed away like his dad taught, limb clutched in both hands so it crossed his chest. A smell like that could mean cougars. A male marking territory. A female with young not ready to travel.

Something to his right caught his eye. A backpacker's fuel cartridge, a refillable one, at the clearing edge that would be the boot's sole. With the branch still extended and the clearing to his back, he moved closer. He prodded the cartridge with his boot toe, saw the dent, the dying vegetation beyond it. Must have sprung a leak, burned the ground cover. Careless hiker. He stooped to pick it up, eyes still working the area, and caught another whiff of cat pee. He dropped the cartridge, a Coleman, and backed away.

Put the limb back where you found it. His dad's voice, not Granny's, sounding a warning. Or reminding him to be cautious, at least. He returned the sawed off branch to the blind, walked backward like he had from the fuel cartridge, his eyes scanning, his ears listening for sounds that didn't belong in the forest. Nothing. When he reached mid-clearing, he turned around.

At the far edge of the clearing, he began descending to the wagon trail, goose bumps on his arms, sweat dripping down his sides. His gut told him he'd found another human camp, not just a fuel container tossed by a guy hiking the ridge.

By the time he reached the wagon trail, his brain said meth, not cougar pee. His eighth grade class had watched a film that showed signs of meth labs. Houses where drapes were never opened, scattered garbage, plastic bottles with holes in them, all sorts of household chemicals. And burn pits where meth makers dumped waste. That dead spot at the edge of the clearing could have been toxic remains of meth, not spilled butane or propane.

He checked in with Vesta, went to his room to shower, and took time to send Ian an e-mail.

Hey, Ian, something came up that I'd like to talk about when you have time.

That forest scene bothered him like a sliver stuck in a finger bothers until it gets dug out. The beach camp guy could have moved into the woods where he had a view of Vesta's without the worry of beachcombers snooping around. "Meth mouth?" he said. "Are you out there?"

Saturday morning Kyra and her mom arrived with a dish full of crystals and an instruction sheet that showed a guy stretched out on the floor, on his back, with rocks lined up from his neck to down below his belly button. There Romar stood, dish and instructions in hand, customers needing coffee and muffins and scrambled eggs. Vesta rescued him. He knew from what she said that she could read him like Granny could.

"Kyra, put those rocks in the back room for now. Romar's up to his eyebrows in work, can't you see? He needs quiet time if those things are going to do any good, and he's not likely to get that with you around. You're like the spark that set the world on fire this morning."

"That's because school's out for the summer, so he and I can get started on my algebra lessons. We can work in the shelter or on the beach."

Leila said, "Hold on, Kyra. You'll be watching the twins."

"Mom." Kyra stretched the word into four syllables.

"Take care of your sisters or sign on for maid work at the motels. Romar will have to come to our place when Vesta gives him a day off."

"By the time he gets to our place, he'll need to turn around and head back," Kyra said.

The door chime sounded. Vesta said, "Hush, now, both of you."

That's how things went for most of the day. Romar checked his email every time he got a break long enough to run down to his room, but all he got was *No new messages*.

During a lull in the late afternoon Vesta went to her office to do paper work and Leila brought out the crystals. They sat at the cafe table farthest from the door. First Leila schooled him in which ones to use if his legs cramped up now that he was hiking into the wilderness. There were several, but she said to try hematite first, and to carry some with him in his pockets.

"Remember the aventurine I gave you before?" she asked, and went right on talking without giving him time to answer. "It had hematite in it, but not enough. This is the pure stuff, okay?"

"Okay," he said, wondering if there were crystals to prevent fear of stupid humans using drugs.

Leila got into spiritual energy next, and chakras, all of which went past him, thanks to Kyra, who sat beside him. She placed crystals in his hand and watched his face for reactions. He could have told her his reactions had nothing to do with pretty rocks.

"Kyra, can you find something else to do for five minutes," Leila said. "I'm trying to cleanse his aura, and you're messing it up. Romar, I think there's something worrying you. Something new since last week when you talked to your uncle and aunt."

"Mom, you're not really a psychic, you shouldn't mess with that stuff."

"I'm sensitive to certain things. Now, go dust grocery shelves or something."

Romar's stomach grumbled. He felt his face heat up.

Kyra said, "He's just hungry, Mom. Why don't you fix him a sandwich?"

"Just go for a minute," Leila said.

The door opened, and there stood Ian.

It was after eight before Ian and Romar made it downstairs.

"Sorry about not answering your e-mail," Ian said. "I've been in Eugene, checking out a few things with an old attorney friend."

"It's not a computer problem," Romar said. "It's something I found in the wilderness area across the highway." He told Ian about the clearing, the downed branches, the smell that could be animal but might be human.

Ian studied the topo map. "You were in a good mile. Up about six hundred feet. Almost directly across the highway from Vesta's. You could see her place, but from here all we see is a rising wall of trees. Have I got it?"

Romar nodded. "You've got it. It sounds crazy, but I started thinking it could be the same guy that camped on the beach. That maybe he picked that spot so he could . . . you know . . . spy on Vesta's place."

Ian pushed up his glasses and pinched the bridge of his nose. Romar had seen him do that before when he was thinking something through.

"You didn't say anything to Vesta?"

"No way. She thinks I just walked along the old wagon trail."

"Good." Ian narrowed his eyes. "I'd like to check out the spot, see the view for myself. You think you could lead me to the clearing without making me climb straight up the way you came down?"

"We could go in the way I went in. We wouldn't even need to go into the clearing. You'll get a decent view of Vesta's several hundred yards closer to the highway." He dragged in a deep breath. "So, do you think someone could be watching this place?"

"I hope not, but I'd like to be certain. If I can take the topo map and book with me, I'll pinpoint the area for the rangers at the Waldport station. One of them can check it out. They're aware that meth gets made in the national forest."

"Uh, remember that night when I told you and Vesta about the camp on the beach, and seeing something that made me think it was a man I'd seen in the dunes?"

"I remember."

"You and Vesta both did something with your eyes. Like a signal thing. Like you might know something about a guy hanging around. And then the day I first met Kyra and Leila, Kyra said something about Vesta's caretaker, and the two women did the same thing."

Ian took off his glasses and rubbed his entire face. "You're observant."

"Yeah, it's from basketball training. Watch the other guys' eyes so you know what they're setting up."

"Okay, Vesta's had some cause for concern. Let's leave it at that for now."

Romar remembered his granny saying, "I'm of two minds." It hadn't made much sense until now. He needed to find his mother, which meant leaving Vesta's, at least for a time. But he couldn't leave Vesta alone if someone was spying on her place.

Not that he could protect her place from someone crazy on meth. He could have taken down the man in the dunes, if it had come to a physical fight. Someone riding a meth high would be another matter.

That Sunday morning he could smell breakfast before he opened the cafe door, and wondered why anyone would ever want to leave. Vesta had sausages heating, waffles baking and coffee ready.

"Come grab a bite before we get busy. I'd forgotten yesterday that they're having Tidepools Discovery Days at Cape Perpetua this weekend. No wonder we were swamped."

"Tidepools?" He'd read about them, but he'd never seen one. He was still more a person of the forest and river than of the ocean and beaches, but he would learn to be both.

"Not out here." Vesta waved an arm. "Our beach is too sandy. You'd have to go a mile or two north to the rocky areas. Maybe you and Kyra can take a break before the tide changes."

It turned out no one got a break until late afternoon, when Vesta closed the restaurant. He was cleaning the kitchen when Kyra grabbed his hand, sending tingles up his arms. He'd shaved that morning but it felt like his whiskers poked straight out. It turned out she was just giving him her address.

"Mom says we've got to get home to rescue Grandma Salty from the twins. Here's directions to our house. Auntie Gram says you can get off around one Wednesday. See you then."

"Right. Around one. Or two, I guess, by the time I get there." He watched her go, wondering if he was of three minds – finding his mother, staying close to Vesta's, and getting away to spend time with Kyra.

When he and Vesta restocked that night, she said, "It gets worse in July and August, but we'll have help from Millie. She cooks for the grade school. She helps me through the busiest part of summer. I'll work out schedules for time off. Wednesdays, after morning rush. Parts of most weekday afternoons. Will you be okay with that?"

"Uh, yeah. I mean . . ." He figured she must be a mind-reader for sure, judging from what she said next.

"I'll arrange for extra help so Salty — my sister — can drive you up to that prison in Washington to meet your mother, once we have that figured out. I don't want you to head up there without knowing how you're getting inside the place." She sighed her tired sigh. "I'd like to drive you up there myself. I'd like to be the one meeting your mother along with you. Like as not, it's better to send you with Salty."

"Why?" he asked, his brain busy with *meet* his mother, not *find* her.It made sense. She wasn't lost, at least not as in missing.

"Salty's better at holding her tongue," Vesta said.

Ian showed up on Monday afternoon, told Vesta he wanted a look at the old wagon trail Romar talked about, and accepted a couple bottles of water to take on their hike. True to his word, they stopped on the old road. Ian took pictures with a digital camera. "Not bad," he said. "Lead the way."

They followed the deer trail Romar used going in on Friday afternoon. Ian stopped every few feet to photograph their surroundings and the changing view of Vesta's by the Sea, the highway and the ocean beyond. He didn't say much, just grunted at steep spots and 'Hmm'd' every few minutes. They made it to the clearing, inspected the downed fir branches without disturbing them, sniffed the air. The pee smell lingered. Ian pulled out a handkerchief and blew his nose.

Romar breathed in a deep whiff and tripped over his big feet trying to step back. His dad's hiking boots squeezed his toes, but he didn't mind all that much. It was like having his dad along. The stench stung his eyes. He pulled his tee shirt up over his nose. Maybe he should carry a handkerchief like Ian did. Granny used to poke an ironed white square in his pocket before he left the house. *"I don't want to see slime tracks on your sleeves, Romie."*

He crossed the clearing to the spot where he'd found the fuel cartridge. "It's gone," he said, "but you can see the dead vegetation."

Ian took the small camera out of his pocket. "One ranger and a volunteer planned to hike in yesterday afternoon or this morning. They may have picked it up. I'm going to shoot a panorama, then some close-ups with you in the frame for height perspective. Don't want to make the climb again, don't want to forget what I'm seeing."

Ian's voice boomed, maybe announcing their presence to anyone lurking out of view. Romar's hand went to his right hip where he carried his dad's knife. Ian had glanced at it and nodded, so Romar pulled it out and held it ready to stab anything that came their way.

When they got back to Vesta's, she said, "How far did you two make it? The whole mile?"

While Romar tried to sort out her question, Ian said, "Most of that. There's a good view. Must have been a bumpy ride, though, in those old wagons."

"My husband liked to poke around over there," Vesta said. "Along Cummins Creek and in the wilderness. I always figured a cougar would get him one day. He carried a gun."

"Not a bad idea," Ian said. "You got any fresh cookies? Cup of coffee?"

Romar got into the game without waiting for Coach Vesta to call the play. "I'm all over that, soon as I wash the pitch off my hands." No need to talk about smells that could be a cougar, or could be meth.

While he scrubbed with powdered cleanser, he wondered what Ian knew and wasn't telling. And what Vesta guessed when she looked at them.

14

AMBER, JADE AND SALTY

Two days later Romar borrowed Vesta's bike to visit Kyra. That left Vesta alone with Millie. Not a good plan, in his thinking, but Ian told him to carry on; forest service rangers and state police were keeping a close eye on the area.

He coasted across the Yachats River Bridge and around the bend into town. Kyra's directions said to go through the village, past the cemetery, up the hill and right where the road ends. He took his time, worked to get his head in the game at hand, not on worries about someone spying on Vesta's place. There stood Kyra, on the porch of a small white house with a shutter dangling from one hinge on an upstairs window.

The house needed paint. So did houses on both sides of it. One had a basketball hoop with rotting string posted above the garage door. His arms ached to take a shot. Saliva filled his mouth. He shook his head. Next thing he'd be drooling over both a rusty hoop and a pretty girl.

Kyra came down the steps. "I saw you coming. Be warned, the twins are dressing up for you."

The screen door banged open and two girls with long dark hair squeezed through side by side. Though Romar had seen girls in strange outfits at Roseburg High, he'd never seen anything like these two. Their skirts dragged. One girl stepped on the hem of hers, stepped back, lifted it and tried again.

They had scarves draped around their necks, wrapped around their heads and tied around their wrists. They'd tucked scarves into their waistbands and let them hang down over their skirts. One and then the other flipped those scarves so they caught the breeze.

They wore lipstick and stuff on their eyelids. Both had chunky crystal necklaces and bracelets like their mother wore.

Kyra said, "Romar Jones, meet Amber and Jade. They're visiting from Romania, where they'd better get back to before their grandmother discovers all her scarves missing."

"You're not s'posed to call her grandmother," one twin said.

The other added, "Besides, she's having her beauty sleep so we have to stay away."

"Yeah, cuz she drank half a bottle of sherry."

"That was s'posed to be put into our sherry cake."

"Which she hardly ever makes."

"It's an excuse to have sherry in the house."

"Which she drinks."

"For her nerves."

"That's because the two of you drive her crazy," Kyra said. "Now get yourselves cleaned up, fold Salty's scarves and put mom's jewelry back where you found it."

One of the girls pointed at a small house next door. "That's Romania," she said.

"It used to be a chicken house in the old days," the other added. They turned and went back inside, shoulder to shoulder.

"A chicken house?" Romar said.

Kyra shrugged. "Grandma Salty calls it the carriage house. She reads a lot of old novels. Mom calls it the old woodshed where they hatched baby chicks one year. The twins say whatever gets them attention."

"Dressed like they were, they wouldn't need to say a thing."

"They get away with it. They get away with pretty much anything since their dad disappeared on that crab boat. Mom tries to make up to them for not having a dad."

"What about you? You said you don't know your dad."

"See, that's the difference. They had a dad they knew, so they've suffered more." Kyra's hands were back on her hips. "Some days I think cleaning rooms at one of the motels or lodges would be easier than dealing with them. And if I don't pass algebra, that's where I'll be stuck the rest of my life."

Kyra's frown and the set of her mouth made Romar grin. "Want to apply algebra formulas to your choices?"

"I better learn how to solve the ones in the assignments. Even Salty's on my case about failing a subject. That's like major big time trouble. Everyone, including Auntie Gram Vesta, says Salty lets us get away with too much."

Romar leaned Vesta's bike against the steps and followed Kyra into the house. Kitchen to the right with a table and chairs by the window that looked out on their drive and houses across the street. No view of the ocean, though it was only a few blocks away.

A glass dish filled with polished stones sat in the middle of the table. Quartz crystals lined up on the windowsill caught and refracted the light. They reminded him of a time he'd gotten into his dad's rifle shells and lined them up. Granny said he'd given her a heart attack, playing with live ammunition.

Kyra dropped an algebra book and notebook paper on the table. "We'll work here. Good vibes. I washed all the crystals this morning so they'd emit supreme energy."

"Good," Romar said. "I mean, I've never taught anyone how to do algebra so crystals might help. Right?"

"Absolutely, if you trust them." Kyra opened the book to chapter four – Graphing Linear Equations and Functions. "I got through the first three chapters before I gave up.

"Why give up then? That should have been far enough to be getting it."

"Because of the teacher. He's okay with guys, but he's clueless when it comes to certain girl things."

"Oh," Romar said, girl things running through his head. "Maybe all guys are. Clueless." That's what Ian Gallagher seemed to think.

They worked for two hours, maybe getting in one hour's worth of study if they subtracted the time spent dealing with the twins' interruptions. Romar wrote out a problem based on that and saw a smile soften Kyra's face for the first time since they'd sat down at the table.

"We're solving for 'x' which represents the minutes you spent focused on algebra, not on the twins or crystals or scarves or jewelry."

"Or talking about Salty, who's heading this way from Romania right this minute."

"Why Romania?"

"Oh, she quotes some sort of poem that ends with '*and I am Marie of Romania*' whenever the twins try to get something by her. She says it's satire that means she's not that dumb."

Romar turned, but not in time to see anyone outside. Then the door swung open on a woman with a face that looked a lot like Vesta's only with wider hair around it. If hair could be wide. The clothes were way different. Vesta wore white shirts with short sleeves, a white apron and khaki slacks. This Vesta look-alike wore a top something like sumo wrestlers wrapped around their fat bodies before they stripped down and tried to choke or smother an opponent to death. Hers had all sorts of colors Granny had told him didn't go together . . . red, orange, purple, pink, yellow, turquoise, green. With glittery things stuck here and there.

She wore shiny black pants tucked into shiny black boots with crystals dangling from the top edge and a clear prism mounted on the toe. And she had hair held down with an Indian headband. Three feathers poked up from the back of her head. They looked like seagull feathers he saw on the beach.

The woman said, "I've come to see Vesta's dear boy."

The minute the door opened, Romar had pushed away from the table to help Kyra with her chair, a wasted gesture since she'd scooted out while his big feet were bumping into table legs.

"Ah, there you are. Now, let me get a close look at you. Kyra, my sweetest child, take this cake and find some plates."

She handed off a shopping bag with an aroma that made Romar's stomach growl. She walked up close to him – so close that his eyes crossed. Her eyes had even brighter lights than Vesta's. They looked like someone had cut off the tips of quartz prisms and set them in the center. Maybe Vesta's looked the same this close. She'd hugged him, but she'd never pushed her bazooms, or whatever they were properly called, up against his chest.

"Oh, my dear boy, except for your eyes and those spectacles, you're the spitting image of Essie when she was a girl. You're taller, of course. Your grandfather was a tall man. That's how he won Essie away from the Yachats' boys. Tall, and he walked straight ahead, not like he was still on the deck of a fishing boat."

Kyra, frowning, stood with the shopping bag in front of her. "You didn't give me a chance to make proper introductions."

The twins swooped in like two seagulls with their eyes on a stranded fish.

"Sherry cake."

"You didn't get drunk after all."

"Or pass out."

"You really baked."

"Don't I bake you naughty girls a cake or cookies every week? Now, you march your behinds over to my house and put all my stolen scarves back where they belong. I had to wear my beaded headband today because I couldn't find one decent piece of silk in the entire house."

"Romar, I'm honored to present Salena Jarvi, known to friends and family as Salty. Before she and my mom got into crystals, they were into beading authentic Native American headbands."

"True, and we sold more than a few before some tribal leaders came through our village and made a fuss."

"Did you bring whipped cream?" Amber asked. Or maybe it was Jade.

"Not for girls who have my lovely silk scarves hidden with other booty they've stolen from Romania."

Amber and Jade giggled, ran off to the back of the house and returned with the scarves.

"March them home," Salty said, her arm out straight, pointing the way. The open end of her sleeve dipped below her knees. The sleeve's inside was shiny red. Silk, he guessed.

Kyra had the cake, whipped cream and plates on the kitchen counter. "Would you like tea, Salty?"

"Absolutely, dear. Earl Grey, please. And a sprinkle of nutmeg atop my whipped cream as usual."

"Romar? Tea?" Kyra asked.

"Uh, sure." He liked tea well enough, thanks to Granny, and he'd accept anything offered to get at the cake.

"When the twins come back, give them thick slices of cake with mounds of whipped cream, and send them to the living room to watch a video," Salty said. "So we can talk about our trip to Washington."

Kyra set placemats and napkins, and served their cake and tea. Romar waited for Salty to take a bite before he lifted his fork. He was almost drooling from the smell. Mounded whipped cream melted a bit on the still warm cake. Salty lifted her teacup. So did Kyra. He followed suit, hoping he was catching on to their ritual.

"To our trip to Washington," Salty said. "I've spoken with an information officer at the prison. Romar, you and I will need to complete some forms they're mailing. We need to be on your mother's approved visitors' list to get in. That takes some time. Until that's all cleared, I think you should start writing to her. I have information on how to address the letter. It has to include her official number."

"Write?" said Romar, who'd written dozens of letters, all of them in the bottom of his dad's pack. Writing to a ghost mother was easy enough. Sort of like writing in a journal. Mostly notes to himself about what he'd like to know about her.

"Send her a picture with a letter. That's permitted. And you'll need a picture ID to get inside." Salty leaned close and squinted.

Romar nodded. He had a mouthful of cake that he needed to swallow and a throat full of worries in the way.

"I know what," Kyra said, "I'll take your picture at Vesta's, out on the beach. You can send your mom that with a letter that says 'This is me.'" She smiled at him and the cake slid down. He didn't have any trouble with the next bite, or the next after that.

The twins brought their empty plates to the kitchen to ask for seconds. When Kyra and Salty both said no, they dipped their fingers into the whipped cream. Kyra got up. They ran out of the room. A minute later they were back with a blue vinyl ball made to look like a basketball.

"Kyra says you're like really good at basketball."

"So we want you teach us how to shoot."

"Cuz we'll be in sixth next year."

"And there's a girls' team."

"And we want to be the best."

"A double threat," they said together and did a high five.

"We can use the neighbor's hoop."

Romar looked at Kyra. He wanted to talk. He wanted to say, "I helped you with algebra so how about you help me write a letter to my mother." He took the ball. It didn't have the right weight or feel, but something happened in his body. His legs were ready for the dance, his shoulders and arms for the shot.

"Maybe next time," Kyra said to the twins. "Romar needs to get back to Auntie Gram's."

"Maybe a few shots," Romar said. "But not in those clothes."

The twins ran off to change. Salty went back to her small house. Kyra gave him a quick kiss at the corner of his mouth.

"You're a nice guy, Romar. I know you're worried about the trip to see your mother. And other things. You don't need to take on the twins."

They were back, in shorts and tee shirts, barefooted, dirty and worn cross trainers in their hands. "Uh huh, he said a few shots," they said in unison.

"How do they do that?" he asked, but Kyra just shrugged.

He stayed another hour, left sweaty and with the imprint of Kyra's lips on his. Another quick kiss, more promising than the first. Good enough to take away worries about letter writing. And about the trip to Washington, now being planned without any input from him.

15

RV Guests

Romar rode the high of Kyra's kiss straight down to the ocean, to Smelt Sands Beach, where he could have a talk with his granny. He sat close to the water. Moisture seeped through his pants and sent a chill up his spine. He scooped up tiny rocks in both hands, and folded his upper body over his legs so people walking by on the trail above the beach couldn't hear him whispering.

"Granny? Are you listening? There's a girl here, in Yachats, that I like. Her name is Kyra Jarvi. She doesn't know anything about her dad, not even his name. Her granny is Salena Jarvi. Did you send me out here to meet Salena? Did you know she'd take me to meet my mother?"

Waves washed over sandstone that jutted out into the ocean, leaving tiny waterfalls that disappeared under the next wave. Wind lifted his hair like Granny's fingers had when she gave it a trim. Spray from a wave washed his face. "Granny?" he said, and there she was, in his head, saying everything would work out. He kept her in his head on the climb to the top of the cape and the wild ride down to Vesta's by the Sea.

The front row of the RV Park, empty when he left, had filled. Seven slots. Two more rigs waited at the entry gate. Romar rode across Vesta's parking lot, jumped off the bike to run it down the grassy slope, and leaned it against the wall beside his door. He dug out his key, went inside to change clothes, splash water here and there and comb his hair.

"Good," Vesta said when he opened the door. "You're just in time. I sent Millie home around four and then, all of a sudden things got busy. Summer Solstice tomorrow. I'd forgotten how many folks come out to worship. This group's a day early according to my calendar."

"Worship?" Romar said, wondering if that's what he'd been doing at Smelt Sands Beach.

"Like the Druids at Stonehenge. To celebrate the sun on the longest day of the year. Last year our beach was crowded even though it rained."

"Druids?" He couldn't keep up with the conversation.

A voice from somewhere in the grocery section said, "Romar? Is that you? It is you!"

He spun, putting his back to Vesta who went on about Druids. He'd heard of them, maybe in a history class, maybe in a 'Once upon a time' story Granny read to him. "Mrs. Matlock?" he said, though he thought of her as Julie.

Julie Matlock wrapped her arms around him and kissed his cheek. It took him a couple seconds to get with the program. He hugged her back like he hoped to hug Kyra one of these days. Julie's hug felt good. Nothing like the hug from Salty, though he hadn't minded that, either.

"Mat and the boys will be so excited. I'm so surprised to see you. We had no idea you'd be here when we decided to pull in for the night. We looked for you around Florence. Mat was checking out a spot there, but it's on the river and he really wants to be on the ocean."

"A spot?"

"A resort spot. Mat's always checking out places. We're on our way to Newport, but the boys were driving us nuts, so we decided on the spur of the moment to stop. I was just telling the owner that she's not listed in the guide."

"The guide?" How many question-answers did that make? He couldn't think fast enough to carry on a conversation. Giving dumb answers, feeling like an idiot stuck in the grocery section with his back to Vesta. He'd caught a quick glance at the clock. Could it be going on six?

"You know, the mile-by-mile guide. Like the one I gave you."

"Oh, yeah. Uh, did you meet Vesta?" Dumb and dumber. Hadn't Julie just mentioned talking to the owner? He turned around so he could see Vesta and the people waiting at the cafe counter and the clock. Five minutes to six.

Vesta smiled. "We met. Give the folks waiting at the gate a hand with hookups at Fourteen. The rig behind them wants Eight. Then we'll need to do some cooler restock and get a fire going in the shelter. Maybe make a few sandwiches."

Good. He wasn't being benched for delay of game. "Got it," he said to Vesta and "Later," to Julie Matlock.

Yeah, later, when he'd have to tell the Matlocks the truth about why he was at Vesta's. They'd given him a ride without knowing he was a runaway. Well, a good riddance run-away as far as Uncle Sherman and Aunt Joan were concerned. Legally on his own, almost, thanks to Ian and Vesta. Maybe that would help.

Julie had guessed he wasn't old enough to carry wine in his backpack. But she hadn't guessed the high-school dropout part, or the mother in prison part. For some reason, he didn't want Julie Matlock to know that his mother was in prison.

The couple waiting at the gate looked too old to drive a motor home. To drive at all, for that matter. The man wore two pairs of glasses, one over the other. "I want number fourteen, and I want to drive straight in. No backing up, you understand?"

"Yes, sir."

"You just lead the way and I'll creep along behind, you understand?"

"You want me to walk you in?"

"That's right. Not too fast. No need to run."

Romar went through the gate, turned left, then right when he'd passed the number eight slot. No rigs in the eight to fourteen row yet and none in the back row, fifteen to twenty. The motor home turned wide, almost hitting fifteen's utility stand, then straightened, its engine growling at Romar's back. He walked a little faster. The horn blast slowed him down. He turned and walked backward the length of the fourteen slot, using hand and arm motions to ease the rig into place.

"Okay, son, now hook us up," the man yelled through the rig's open window. "Electricity and TV first, there's a program the missus likes. Make it snappy."

Romar could almost feel his eyebrows knitting and wondered if they would collide above his nose. "Yes SIR," he said. Coach taught him to answer like that. "When someone talks down to you or orders you around, put some power into sir. Works better than a fist without the trouble."

The rig that had been waiting behind Fourteen was in place at slot eight, the driver walking toward him. He stopped too close to where Romar was working. "We're ready to be hooked up soon as you get through here."

A voice behind him said, "Romar Jones. Julie said she'd found you. We looked around Florence."

And two younger voices calling, "Romar, Romar, Romar."

"Mr. Matlock," Romar said, taking Mat's extended hand. "Hunter. Preston."

Preston carried sand dollars in both hands. "I found these on the beach," he said. "They have doves inside."

"They do?" Romar didn't know anything about sand dollars except that they crunched when he stepped on them.

A voice from inside Fourteen shouted, "Hey, we need our water hooked up."

Eight said, "Just give me the key to unlock the utilities. I'll hook myself up."

Romar looked at the man like he'd look at a basketball player trying to drive past him. "I'll be right with you. Owner's policy. We do the unlocking." That wasn't totally true; Vesta often handed keys over to a guest. His decision had to do with the guy in fourteen.

"Come on, boys," Mat said, "let's wash those shells. Romar, you stop by when you get a break. We're right in front of these folks. Number seven."

Romar finished Fourteen's hookups, knocked on their door and called, "You're good to go." He sprinted to Eight where the man had his hose and electrical cords waiting. He looked half the age of the guy in Fourteen. Maybe less than half. He wore jeans and a sweat shirt with the sleeves pushed up, and sunglasses on top of his head.

"Sorry you had to wait," Romar said.

"No problem. I didn't mean to hassle you, it's just that we were stuck behind that old fart for the better part of an hour. We'd like to get set up."

"Yeah, my boss was alone. Makes it hard." He grabbed the hose while the man plugged in the electric cord.

"Vesta said you were running late. Actually, she said it was your day off, but she thought you'd be back to give her a hand. Said you're the new caretaker."

"Right." Romar opened the water valve, stood and looked at the man again. He had suntan lines along the side of his head and around his eyes, which were squinting. Romar knew about squinting. He was pretty sure the guy squinted to think, not to see.

"You look young to be the caretaker. A lot younger than the one I met here last year."

"It's a summer job," Romar said.

The man handed him a card. "Tom Findlay. Photographer slash journalist, shooting and writing about some of the lesser known spots along the coast. I started a piece on Vesta's place late last summer. Came out to finish it."

"Romar Jones, nice to meet you. I've gotta get back inside, do some restock. Let me know how I can help." He turned, on edge from how the guy studied him. The guy transmitted a message, or a question Romar couldn't get.

He sprinted through Vesta's door, slowed to smile at her, and slipped inside the cleaning closet to wash his hands.

"I still haven't gotten the cooler and snacks restocked," Vesta said when he stepped into the kitchen, wrapping and tying an apron. "Take a sandwich to eat while you're working. Soon as it's quiet I'll tell you about the guy in Eight."

"Check," he said around the sandwich he'd had in his hand before Vesta told him to take one. It came from a plate set in his usual place.

Two big sandwiches, salad on the side, cup and glass ready for whatever he chose to drink. Vesta took good care of the caretaker. So, why did the last one leave? And why did the photographer in eight give him that long look?

He did two more hookups, rang up snack and drink purchases – including beer and wine, as if he could do that legally – got the fire going in the shelter, and pushed up his glasses about a hundred times. Nervous habit. They weren't slipping.

"Sorry about this day getting ahead of me," Vesta said during a lull. "You didn't get a proper half day off and tomorrow could be worse."

"It's okay. I should have come right back after helping Kyra with algebra."

"Instead of teaching the twins how to shoot a basketball?" Vesta said, the lights in her eyes twinkling. "They called here. Millie answered. They told her it was urgent. I grabbed the phone, ready for bad news, and there the twins were, both talking at once. 'Romar's cute, Auntie Gram. Can we come help you so he can give us more basketball lessons?' I told them they'd just taken a year off my life and hung up."

"Um, well, after helping the twins I stopped at Smelt Sands to say hi to Granny."

Vesta patted his arm like she'd been doing almost from the minute he first walked into her place. "I was only a little worried."

"Because of traffic? And the bike? And not getting back by four like I said?" His granny admitted to worrying if he ran late. She had a long list of things she thought could happen to him when he was out of her sight.

Vesta nodded, shrugged, swiped a wet cloth across the counter. "Women tend to worry."

"Oh," Romar said, maybe getting it. "I wouldn't take off without telling you." He looked for a wet cloth of his own, for something to do. "I like it here. You're really good to me." That statement was like tossing an air ball, no points for a wild shot.

"It's a lot to expect of someone young as you. Long work hours, so much responsibility, all of us poking into your private life. Loading you down with crystals to make you feel better. As if."

"That's okay. The work's not hard, the food's great, the crystals are pretty." He gave her his best grin, worth at least one point.

Vesta stopped wiping the counter. "I've been thinking about putting this place on the market in a year or two. Got to thinking more this afternoon when Tom Findlay showed up. He started working on a write-up last summer. I suspect Ian asked him to come back, maybe work on a layout for a real estate magazine. Ian can get a bit pushy."

Romar nodded. "He told me he thinks you should sell."

"Eventually. The price has to be right. Places like this . . . an old building with an old campground . . . don't have much appeal these days. I'd hate to see it all bulldozed down for a condo."

Romar thought about Granny when they had to leave the Glide house, how she'd said the house needed someone to love it like she had. "Oh," he said, hoping his brain would come up with something to make Vesta feel better. Sometimes talking was like writing poetry. You needed time to find the right words.

She raised her head and looked at him.

"The thing is, I'd like you to stick with me, live here with me until I leave and then move with me wherever I go. Yachats or Waldport, I'm not sure." She looked down at her cleaning cloth and then back at him. "It might not be right, with your granny so recently dead, but I just feel like you could be my own grandson. You could think of me as your stand-in grandmother. You know, a substitute, so to speak. I'd never replace your granny, but I could stand in now and again."

Romar struggled to swallow. He looked down, like something on the floor needed attention. "You mean you'd remind me to get a haircut and wash my socks?"

Being alone with only the pack on his back gave him a taste of loneliness that went beyond the sadness of death, first his dad and then Granny. He'd had plenty of time to think about the difference between living in a nice house and living in a home where he was welcome. Granny had been unhappy at Uncle Sherman's too. Leaving there with a few of her ashes in his pack freed her spirit from that house. He should have left the day after basketball season ended.

Now Vesta was offering to be his granny and he got choked up, skinny arms hanging off his body when they could be wrapped around Vesta. He'd hugged Salty and then Julie, but now he stood frozen, like a player hanging on to the ball, afraid to take a shot. Bzzzt. Jones chokes.

He could use another granny – one that wasn't dead.

"Stick with me, but go to school." Vesta said. "That could mean living away during the week, like we talked about before."

He nodded. The door blew open, chiming and banging all at once. Hunter and Preston Matlock shoved and tripped their way inside.

Preston elbowed Hunter and got to Romar first. "Mom said to ask if you want to make S'mores with us. In the shelter. There's a fire going, and she said the coals are getting good, and we've got sticks and marshmallows and stuff. Only we could use some more chocolate."

"If you're not closed," Hunter said. "She said to make sure you're not already closed. I've got money."

"You've come to the right place," Vesta said. "Romar, grab some of those Hershey bars and go help the boys keep their marshmallows from burning."

16

VESTA'S SHELTER

Clouds drift across the sun as it drops toward the sea. Those words formed in Romar's head and joined all the unspoken ones he wanted Vesta to hear him say. To be accurate, the horizon would soon hide the sun as the earth tilted. Did scientists ever write poetry?

He finished his second S'more and a bottle of water, and plunged his hands into his pockets. Polished aventurine in the right hand pocket to dispel anxiety and fear, according to the information card Leila Jarvi gave him. Sharp amethyst crystals in the left to keep him calm.

He'd gone to his room to grab a sweatshirt and scooped up the polished rock and sharp crystals on his way out. Couldn't hurt. Might help, so Kyra said about the crystals lined up in the Jarvi kitchen window. When he asked how dispelling anxiety and keeping calm differed, and why one crystal couldn't do both, she just looked at him and grinned. Cute little grin. Just thinking about it made heat run up his neck and onto his face.

The cloud layer at the horizon turned pinky orange, the layer above it bright yellow with the sun glistening in its middle. Like a stone on a ring band, he thought. The layer above the yellow had purples and pinks mixed together with bits of yellow sneaking in here and there. He wondered if he could get an acceptable description out of the view if he tried.

Acceptable to Whitley. Pinky orange, yellow and purple worked fine for him. The water all the way to the horizon was stirred up, not rough like whitecaps, but not smooth like glass. It had a reddish path that stretched from the setting sun to the shore.

He gave up on description and listened to Vesta talking to Julie Matlock. Mat was off sipping wine with a couple who sat at the far edge of the shelter. Julie and the Matlock boys had mugs of hot chocolate.

Romar kept his attention on the boys and their roasting sticks, though he wanted to watch Julie's reaction to Vesta's story.

"His grandmother and my older sister were related by marriage," Vesta said. "Luck made him stop here on his way to Smelt Sands Beach. That and an empty stomach."

Julie Matlock said, "We didn't know . . ." He didn't hear what they didn't know and tried to remember what he'd told them. That he was heading for the coast and going north from Reedsport. Not much more.

People on the beach cheered when the sun disappeared. A few minutes later Tom Findlay and a woman, both carrying cameras and tripods, came into the shelter. "Tom and Nora Findlay," Vesta said to Julie, then named the couple sipping wine with Mat.

"We'd like a shot of your boys roasting marshmallows," Tom Findlay said to the Matlocks.

"With your permission," Nora Findlay added. "Just their backs and the roasting sticks. Since we freelance, we never know where our work might appear, so we're careful about photographing faces."

It took five minutes and several clicks of their cameras before the boys quit acting. Romar got it – take plenty of pictures when they're posing and then a couple when they stop. That's how you get a natural. He stepped out of the way when Nora Findlay's look said she had a good one.

Two other couples who'd walked past the shelter on their way up from the beach returned with steaming mugs. Romar ran a quick count – fourteen people counting Vesta and himself. He gave up trying to sort out conversations. He'd talk to Julie Matlock in the morning. Mat, too. They deserved to know the truth about him. He turned when Vesta said, "Will that be okay with you, Romar?"

"Huh?" he said, and felt his face heat up again. "I mean, what?" Granny said 'huh' shouldn't even be in the dictionary.

"Tom and Nora would like to take some pictures of your room, and the laundry room and dungeon. To do a complete layout."

"Tomorrow morning, not tonight," Tom said.

"Sure," Romar said, surprised to be asked. "I'll make the bed and pick up my clothes. And sweep the laundry room floor, it's a little sandy."

"The dungeon, too?" Tom asked. "Okay to take shots in there, Romar?"

"That's up to Vesta," he said. "It's really dark, but I keep it in order and all."

"Sounds like you're doing a commercial spread," Mat said.

Tom nodded. "Could serve for that, or for insurance purposes. That's what we freelancers do . . . talk potential customers into covering all their bases while we're on site."

"This site is a perfect resort spot," Julie said. "Low bank, rocks in close and then sand forever, little streams crossing to the water."

Romar's head rotated from one speaker to the other like a basketball player looking for a teammate to block out a defender.

"Not quite perfect, Julie," Mat said. "Not for a marina. We're looking for a spot at a marina."

"You're looking for a marina." A frown wrinkled Julie's forehead for a moment. "I'm looking for a place where the boys can get on the beach. This is a perfect place for families. Think about it. Vesta could turn this shelter into a club house, maybe put a hot tub right next to the opening, build cabanas alongside the RV hookups."

"Cabanas?" Mat said. "On the Oregon Coast? Where it rains ten months of the year?"

"Yes, Mat. Where better to have a covered area that gives families more room when they're parked."

"Park model cottages," Nora Findlay said. "We did a layout for a resort like that. They call their place an RV Condo. They sell the sites, but most of them are available for rent through the resort manager."

"Exactly," Julie said. "Mat, you should talk to your board." She turned to Vesta. "Mat's business invests in places like this, but he's got his mind set on getting to Newport so he can scope out another marina. He doesn't know how hard it is to keep the boys entertained in an RV while he's out in the middle of the ocean."

"I'm not ready to sell," Vesta said.

Julie, who'd again been frowning at Mat, turned to Vesta and smiled. "I'm sorry, I'm being pushy. Mat can leave his contact information. If you decide to sell someday, you can get in touch."

"Selling will be a big step for me," Vesta said, her eyes moving from Julie and Mat to the photographers and then to Romar. "Romar's being here makes staying much easier."

"What a great summer job you found," Julie said. "Was it just good luck? I mean, did you just stop by to see if Vesta had an opening, or did you see an ad somewhere?"

"Good luck. I sort of stumbled in here during a rain storm."

"Destiny, pure and simple," Vesta said. "You might say we were waiting for him to come by. Or hoping. My sister, especially. She'd had a Christmas card and note from his grandmother. The note said she hoped she and her grandson could make a summer trip to Smelt Sands Beach, where she grew up. Then, in late March, we heard she'd died. And then, before he got as far as Yachats, he came through my door."

"Oh, Romar, I'm sorry about your grandmother," Julie said.

He swallowed. Gulped, really. The whole place got quiet. Even Hunter and Preston quit talking. The last color was fading from the sky. Soon the horizon wouldn't be visible, but the waves' crash and lull and crash again would remind them that an ocean was just beyond view. The ocean his granny loved. The ocean sounds he'd miss if they stopped.

"Granny wanted part of her ashes to come back out here." He spoke to Julie but looked at his feet, just in case her sympathy made him choke up. "So, that's where I was heading when you met me on the river."

"Have you already scattered her ashes?" Julie asked.

He looked up, noticed her eyes were wet, blinked his own a couple times and nodded. Vesta patted his arm and gave him a look that said maybe he should tell the rest.

"There's a lot I didn't talk about." He pushed at his glasses and almost wished they slid down so he wouldn't have to see faces watching him. "See, my dad was killed in an accident two and a half years ago, so Granny and I had to move from Glide to Roseburg. We lived with my uncle and aunt. Granny's first-born son and daughter-in-law." His eyes went back to his feet. Now he felt embarrassed. No, ashamed. "They didn't really want us, but they didn't think Granny and I could live alone."

"What about your mother?" Julie whispered, like she'd already guessed.

The sky over the ocean still held a little light, not as much as the fire. He stepped away, into deeper shadows, hoping that he could state the truth without sounding and looking mad. "She's in prison. I don't remember her."

Julie gasped. Whatever she'd guessed, it wasn't prison. She covered her mouth with one hand and put an arm around Preston, the son nearest her. Mat's head turned from watching the fire to focus on Romar. Hunter said "Prison?"

Romar watched Julie. Next to Vesta, she was the person most important to him in that group. "She's in Washington, where I really meant to go after leaving Granny's ashes. It's not like I missed her or anything, not while I had my dad and my granny. We didn't even talk about her very much. I tried to keep it quiet in Roseburg . . . in school. Her being in prison. But the school counselor knew, and some kids heard."

Julie, tears spilling down her face, said "Oh, Romar, that's not fair. That's just not fair."

"Life's not fair, Julie, we all know that," Mat said.

Romar thought he sounded mad. That made sense. Most guys acted mad to keep from acting sad or sorry. Then Mat moved to Romar and dropped an arm across his shoulders and that about blew it for Romar hiding his feelings.

"You've had some tough breaks. Do you mind my asking . . . I've been wondering ever since we dropped you off . . . anyway, if you don't mind telling us, I've been wondering how old you are."

"Fifteen," Romar said. Mat's arm felt warm. The shelter had cooled off and was growing dark. The fire could use more wood. "I might as well tell you the rest. I walked out of Roseburg High School the day before I pulled Preston out of the river. But it's all okay because I'm finishing my classes online. Already finished, since we were about at final test time. I owe my English teacher a poem and then a final.

Vesta has a friend who's helping me get into an independent living program."

"And," Vesta said, "if all goes well, he's going to live with me part time and with my friend part time, and go back to school out here."

"After I meet my mother. There's some things I need to sort out."

"How . . . how much longer will she be in prison?" Julie asked.

Romar shrugged and shook his head. "I don't know. I've never talked to her or even had a letter from her."

Julie put her arms around him and squeezed. "That's so sad. I'd adopt you this very minute, but it looks like Vesta beat me to it."

Mat's arm still rested on his shoulder. If they didn't all move and let him fiddle with the fire, he'd probably start slinging snot. He went for his tough act.

"Yeah, well, adoption might not be a good idea. I read some stuff online about kids with parents in prison. This one thing kept coming up. Kids with a parent in prison are at risk of ending up there, too."

"But you had your granny all these years, and your dad through your childhood," Vesta said, the lights in her eyes brighter than the fire's flames. "That makes a difference. My friend Ian looked up those statistics, too. He said you're not going to be one. A statistic, I mean."

"And now you have Vesta and her friend," Julie said. "Plus, Mat and the boys and I will be staying in touch. I've just made an executive decision that we will e-mail you, and we will all be at your high school graduation. Maybe, by then, we'll own part of a place out here somewhere."

Romar opened his mouth, but nothing came out before Mat said, "Don't even bother to protest. When Julie makes an executive decision, it's set in concrete."

Nora Findlay came around from the far side of the fire. "Romar, I know you and Vesta have work to do inside, but I want to say how moved I am by hearing your story. After you've met your mother, if it feels right to you, I'd like to write an article about your journey. We wouldn't have to use your name. There must be lots of other kids with parents in prison."

"Over two million and rising every day," Vesta said. "Maybe ten million when you add those whose parents are out but under legal supervision."

"Dear God," Julie said. "I had no idea."

"Yeah," Romar said, "I didn't either until Ian helped me look at some web sites. Mostly kids aren't going to talk about it, but word gets around. Most parents don't want their kids hanging out with a guy whose mother's a criminal."

"That's really really unfair," Julie said. She looked at Mat. "Don't bother with another speech about life not being fair. It all makes me so mad."

Preston eased in alongside Romar. "I'll be your friend, Romar. I like you."

"Thanks, I like you too," Romar said. The sadness ache built behind his eyes. "Hey, I've gotta go finish cleaning up Vesta's kitchen."

He ran up the hill, rounded the corner, sniffed twice and wiped his sweatshirt sleeve across his face, just in case. He wanted his granny to tell him everything would work out. He'd made it to the kitchen and started water running before Vesta came in. She locked the door and turned on the closed sign.

"You're a fine young man, Romar," Vesta said. "Your mother's a fool, wasting her chances to know you. Your granny did right by you and, if you're willing, I'm going to take up where she left off."

"Thanks." He turned off the water, mopped his face with his sleeve one more time and managed a smile before he turned to face Vesta. He composed a speech that would let her know how he felt. Her cheeks glistened with tears. He did the rapid eye blink trick, and sniffed.

"Damn," he said. "No, I don't mean that . . . well, I mean it about sniffing, not about you. What I really mean is . . ." His mouth hung open. Air ball.

Vesta patted his arm. "That's fine, Romie. Thanks is fine. You don't need to say another word, but you need to hear a story I've been keeping from you. It's time you hear the truth about my former caretaker."

17

SUMMER

Truth time, but from Vesta, not him. He closed his mouth and tucked his lips between his teeth, wishing he'd gone for the broom rather than a sink full of water when he first came in. He could clutch a broom, make some moves so she wouldn't expect him to make eye contact.

"About my caretaker and what went on with the Findlays last summer. They had reservations for Labor Day weekend. It's always crazy busy here over Labor Day, and then it gets quiet. Too quiet at times. Give me a minute to sort my thoughts."

Vesta grabbed a cloth and started wiping the counter.

Pregame anxiety swept over him. He rolled his shoulders, drew in a breath and let it out, concentrating on the basket that existed only in his mind. "You don't have to tell me if it makes you sad."

She slapped the cloth on the counter's edge. "It doesn't make me sad, it makes me mad all over again. Not at the Findlays. They were in the area working on photography for a friend who was writing a travel book. During a lull they showed me a photo layout they'd done of a small resort like mine and asked if they could do a shoot of my place, no strings attached. No charge unless I wanted to use some of the photos for advertising or whatever."

Vesta wiped one small spot on the counter over and over.

"I told them that was fine with me. Ian is always after me to do some advertising, but then he's always after me to sell the place, too. I tell him every time that I need to wait for the day when social security will kick in. Just so you know, I'm sixty-three, so that means another two years or so for full benefits.."

"Oh," Romar said. Granny had been in her seventies. He wondered if Vesta had high blood pressure. That had been one of his granny's problems.

"All the photo taking bothered Dalton. My caretaker, Dalton Grimes, did I ever tell you his name?"

"No," he said, wondering why she got caretakers with odd names.

"Both Findlays took lots of pictures, including some of my other guests. They'd print them on a computer setup in their rig and hand them out. Courtesy photos, they called them."

Vesta rinsed her cloth, pulled the plug, refilled the sink with hot water and poured in some bleach. He dipped a cloth for wiping down tables and chairs. Good to be busy.

"Tom Findlay set up a laptop in the shelter and spent a lot of time writing. He'd work at his computer, then take some more pictures, then write again. For some reason, that upset Dalton. They got into a tiff that started in the laundry room. Dalton said the guy was poking his nose into the dungeon where any number of things could be stolen."

Vesta drew in a breath and continued. "'What things?' I asked him. It seems to me my husband left a lot of junk down there in those cabinets. It needs to be sorted one of these days. Anyway, the long and short of it is Dalton and Tom got into a physical struggle. Ian was here at the time. He tried to settle everyone down. He knew I was worried about a lawsuit."

Romar had seen enough fights on school grounds to know there was always someone trying to calm things down. Most of the time the fight moved to another place.

"That was Sunday of the three-day weekend. Coral was here with me. She's my daughter. She'd dated Dalton years ago. That's how I knew him. But she met someone else at college and had a baby. My only grandchild, who's a teenage girl now, was with her dad that weekend, so Coral came out here to give me a hand."

"Oh," Romar said, his tension growing.

"Dalton never got over Coral. He went off to the Gulf War, and came back from that a bigger mess than when Coral broke off with him. I felt sorry for him, which is why I gave him the caretaker's job."

A bigger mess. War. The guy in the dunes said he served the country. It looked like Vesta had a habit of helping guys she felt sorry for.

"Coral and Dalton started arguing about something. She got him outside, away from customers. Away from my hearing, for that matter. When she came back in, she said he went for a walk. We left it at that until a car engine started in the middle of the night. That woke both Coral and me. She guessed before I did that Dalton stole my car. We called the police. They showed up here about eight the next morning. You can guess how that went, with police wanting to ask questions and guests wanting coffee and breakfast. Someone found my poor little car stuck in the sand dunes south of here."

"The dunes?"

"The police found him wandering around half out of his mind. Stoned, they said. He went back to prison, and then he walked away. Escaped. We were worried, Ian and I, that the camp you found down the beach belonged to Dalton. Ian had authorities check that out."

Visualizing a ball and a basket wasn't calming Romar's nerves. He twisted his cleaning cloth until it looked like a rope. "You think he's living out here somewhere? In the woods, maybe, since the beach camp's gone?"

"He's not been seen, so we're hoping he's moved on," Vesta said. "Ian checks with the authorities every day. They don't know if the camp was Dalton's. They seem to think he's left this area."

"That's good." It would be good, but Romar didn't believe it, not after evidence of someone hiding out in the forest across the highway. He'd bet Ian didn't believe it either.

Vesta sighed. "Except now I'm worried he might head for Eugene, where Coral lives. She works for the University of Oregon."

"Have you warned her?" That wouldn't be good, either, but it would probably be harder to hide on a university campus. At least if it was the same ragged, smelly guy from the dunes. He wouldn't exactly fit in with college students and professors.

"Yes, and she's warned campus police. I wanted you to know about the whole mess before you help the Findlays set up to take pictures downstairs. Tom might say something. He's a good man to come back by here again without my asking. I think having a photo layout of this place might come in handy one of these days."

"Uh, does Dalton have a scruffy beard? And dark hair like mine?"

"Certainly no beard when he worked for me. His hair is dark. He's a tad shorter than you, slight of build, though he'd put on a paunch last summer. He could go through a good amount of food."

Romar hadn't realized how tight his teeth were clenched until he relaxed enough to smile. "Yeah, that's easy to do around here. So, what will you do if Dalton shows up?"

"Give him something to eat, if it's during the day. Dial nine-one-one and blow my air horn, if it's at night."

"Okay, if I hear the air horn, I'll know to come running." Romar hoped he'd be there, if the guy showed up. Going off to meet his mother didn't seem quite so urgent. He needed to check some things out with Ian.

Julie Matlock hugged him goodbye before she, Mat and the boys headed for Newport. That got him stirred up, happy and sad all at once. His thoughts jumped from Julie to Kyra to his mother to Vesta to Dalton. Lucky for him, he had plenty of work waiting: the lawn grew a foot overnight; shrubs pushed through the fences and beach stair rails; someone spilled detergent in the laundry room and left white footprints in spite of the sign asking guests to clean up after each use.

He swept and mopped, mowed and clipped, washed his own laundry, and stuck the letter he was supposed to write to his mother in a drawer. So far he'd written *Dear Mother*. It sounded phony. Maybe, if he crossed out *Dear*, he'd find something to say.

He should have asked Julie Matlock to help him. She'd know what a mother would like to hear.

He grabbed a second shower, just in case, before the Findlays started taking pictures inside the building. They took a dozen shots of the caretaker's room, a couple of the laundry, then set up lights in the dungeon.

"This room could be crucial when Vesta decides to sell," Tom said. He slid out drawers on a tall metal tool cabinet. "I'll stagger them so viewers get the idea that they're full of treasures. Wow, a woodworker's paradise. And a mechanic's. Look at all these tools, Nora."

Nora Findlay moved their lights around to get the best angles. Tom tried the handles on the metal cabinet nearest the door but it didn't open.

"Vesta calls that the chemical cabinet," Romar said. "She says it's full of old paint and caustic cleaners her husband used. That's why it's over here, farthest from the furnace. Some of the big cabinets on the other side are locked, too, but all the tools and equipment a caretaker needs are in the open."

"Someone's arranged things in logical order since the last time I stepped in here. Was that you, Romar?"

He felt his face heat up. He needed gardening tools in one place rather than all over the room. "Yeah, somewhat, though Mr. Gallagher told me he'd tried to straighten up the mess the other guy left. You know, the Dalton guy you met last summer."

"An odd duck, that one." Tom aimed his camera at the line of rakes, hoes and shovels. Minutes passed before he added, "I think the guy meant to kill me when I got in here."

"For real?" Romar pictured the guy in the dunes, the beach camp and its stench, the blind in the forest. It had to be the same guy. The Dalton guy. Romar looked around for something to do with the energy that surged through his body. He needed a basketball, an opponent to watch, a teammate moving into position. He needed to do his dribble dance.

"For real for sure," Nora said. "He grabbed one of Tom's cameras and twisted the neck strap. He was breathing hard. Panting, like he'd been running."

Tom said, "I was trying to protect my camera when he picked up a shovel and swung. Nora had her camera on video. We have the whole scene stored on a flash drive. Police have a copy."

Romar moved his feet like he would if he saw a chance to drive the key.

Tom squinted at him. "You do know that he took off later with Vesta's car?"

Romar nodded. "And left it in the dunes, and then got picked up and taken to jail. And then got out."

"He's out?" Nora said. "Oh, my God, he's out, Tom."

Her eyes darkened. Until that moment, Romar thought that only happened in stories.

Tom pulled her in close to him. "Vesta told me, but I didn't want to say anything to you. She said the police think he left the area."

Nora pushed away from Tom, drew in a deep breath and blew it out. "Well, this is interesting. Last night I was thinking about how sad it is when children have parents in prison, wondering if those parents should really be there. Now I'm mad that Dalton's not in prison, and I don't give a damn how many kids he might have fathered."

"Whoa, Nora, take it easy."

Nora shoved her hands onto her hips, elbows out. "You should have told me."

"I was waiting . . ." Tom lifted his shoulders and left them fall. "You're right. I should have told you. I'm sorry."

The Findlays moved into a hug. Romar stood there, wondering what to do. Grab a push broom and sweep away the tension in the room.

"Might be interesting to know what's in those locked cabinets on the far wall," Tom said over Nora's shoulder.

"Yeah," Romar said, trying to get back to the task at hand. "Vesta said she needs to go through them. They're full of her husband's things, some of them saved from his dad." He knew from how she talked about her husband that she still missed him. Ian Gallagher still missed his wife. Maybe Ian and Vesta would get married one day. Take up where their first marriages left off. Kyra hoped they would.

By the time they finished, Romar had learned a lot about photography. Maybe he could write to his mother about lighting and angles and lens filters. But why would she care? Prisoners probably didn't have cameras.

The day settled into normal busy after that. The Findlays disappeared into their rig to download photos and work on layouts. Millie left at two. Ian Gallagher showed up about four.

"Thought you'd need some help, sweetheart. Beaches are crowded all the way down from Waldport. State parks north of here are filling up. I picked up more soup stock."

In the nanosecond before he heard "soup stock," Romar hoped Ian would say "Kyra." He pictured himself and Kyra side by side, waiting for the sun to disappear, counting the minutes until all color faded from the sky and blackness seeped in. Maybe she'd bring an old blanket they could sit on. They would wrap up together when it got dark and chilly.

No such luck. He knew she was stuck on twin watch. He liked the twins, and thought that seeing to them might be fun. They could all shoot hoops.

When Vesta told him to take a break, he headed for the beach. There were kids chasing waves and couples holding hands. Next time he saw Kyra, he'd ask her to walk with him and take her hand. Her small hand would disappear in his big one.

He ran south on packed sand for speed, back high on the beach for muscle building. Someone had pitched a tent near the spot where the smelly camp had been, cleaned out the fire pit and set up driftwood benches. It made a nice setting for watching the sun set.

As he neared the beach stairs he saw the couple from Fourteen coming down. The man with his two pairs of glasses, his big belly leading, then the woman overweight, too, but with only one pair of glasses.

The man stepped onto the beach and reached back for his wife, still two steps up and clinging to the rail. "Come on," he said.

The woman leaned forward, then back, like she was rocking on her feet. Like a teeter-totter, Romar thought. He covered the distance in two long strides, one hand extended to help.

The woman moved one foot, over-stepped, and pitched forward onto the rocks below the last step. She screamed, then moaned. Blood spurted from her nose. For a brief moment, Romar saw Granny with her nose bleeding. It was the last time he'd seen her alive. The woman's scream brought guests from the shelter – a woman and man he didn't recognize.

"Get us some help," Romar shouted to them. It would take two or three strong men to get her up, big as she was. He knelt to start assessing the woman's injuries. Her eyes were open, filled with fear and pain. She kept gasping.

"Easy," he said. "Slow breaths, in and out. Your nose is bleeding. I need to pinch it for you. Where else do you hurt?" Those words came straight from his dad, who'd said them to a guy who'd slipped and hit his head while they were hiking in the Boulder Creek Wilderness.

The woman moaned. Tears ran and mixed with blood.

Romar glanced up at the man he thought of as Fourteen, still standing, clutching the end of the rail. "Can you give me a hand?"

"My knees are shot. You're on your own. This place damn well better have good insurance."

"Huh?" Fourteen's wife was moaning and crying, and he ranted about insurance.

Nora Findlay had started down the stairs. She stopped when the man spoke. "I'll get Vesta,"

"No, get Ian," Romar shouted. "Her friend, Ian Gallagher. And bring a first aid kit."

The woman's blood pooled in two places on the rocks, one from her nose, the other from a gash on her head. Romar tugged off his tee shirt, shoved it under the gash, felt the lump forming. He ran his fingers along the woman's neck until he found her carotid artery. That's what his dad had done. Her pulse pounded. Must be better than a flutter.

"Can you tell me your name?"

"Her name's Iris," Fourteen said. "I'm Earl."

Romar shot Earl a look, not easy to do with his face close to the woman's. "Iris, do you know where you are right now?"

"Shit," Earl said, "she's on the goddamn beach bleeding to death, where do you think she is?"

Several people had run up from the water's edge and gathered behind them. One woman said, "Shut up, you idiot. He's checking her for verbal response."

Adults. Romar wished they would all shut up so he could go through the drill. Name, where are you, what year is this, who's the president. Coach taught that. They had a diabetic kid on their team.

The stairs creaked. Tom Findlay spoke over the chatter. "I can help. I'm trained." He knelt, placed two fingers alongside Romar's on the woman's neck.

"She bumped her head. Right temple. Lump forming."

Tom's fingers moved to check the lump. Ian started down the stairs, cell phone at his ear.

Romar stepped out of the way, more worried about a lawsuit than about Fourteen's wife bleeding on the beach. A lawsuit would be his fault, he was the caretaker. He eyed the steps, the rail. They looked okay, not loose or wobbly.

"Fire department's sending an ambulance," Ian said. "For now, let's make her comfortable as possible."

Romar looked out across the sea, aware of the ocean's roar. He hadn't heard the sound while he focused on Iris. Light rays fanned from behind a cloud layer hovering above the horizon. Gulls squawked. His stomach growled. Must be about seven. Still three hours to go before sunset on the longest day of the year.

18

WORRIES BY THE SEA

While they waited for medics, Ian and Tom worked to make Iris comfortable with blankets and pillows Romar brought from his room. They eased her into a sitting position, iced her head and helped her sip grape juice. Nora talked Earl into going up to the shelter with her.

Romar tucked three polished crystals into Iris's hand. He'd grabbed them from Leila's dish, uncertain what they were called or what they were meant to do. "Hold onto these," he said. "They'll help you calm down, and that helps control the pain."

She took them and smiled. "Why, thank you. They're pretty rocks."

Good, he had Iris smiling, and Nora had Earl out of the picture. The whole incident of Iris's fall replayed in Romar's head like a stuck commercial. Fourteen (he had a hard time thinking of the man as Earl) reached out a hand to help his wife. He said, "Come on," to her, Romar knew that for absolute certain. Then he grabbed her wrist and tugged. Her wrist, not her hand. Iris might have made it to the beach upright if she'd been on the bottom step when Earl decided to grab hold of her.

The next picture in his mind was of Iris glaring at Earl while Earl stood there talking about insurance and suing for damages and medical expenses. The insurance part and the suing part worried Romar.

The ambulance arrived. Earl shouted something at the medics, but he didn't get up from the shelter chair. Romar figured that was the first smart thing he'd done since he decided to take Iris for a walk on the beach.

The medics started an IV and went through their question drill. They got Iris onto the stretcher and up the steps she shouldn't have tried to go down in the first place. Anyone with ankles spilling out over the tops of her shoes would have a problem with steps and rocks and loose sand.

The ambulance driver held the IV and talked to Iris while the other two men carried her. They had sweat running into their eyes and down their necks. Iris had to weigh well over two hundred pounds. It would take two Grannies to make one Iris.

One medic sat in the back of the ambulance with Iris while the other two asked questions about her fall. Earl said she'd slipped on the steps. Romar said only that he saw her fall forward. The ambulance pulled out with its light flashing but no siren.

Ian and Earl followed in Ian's car. Romar took a shower, his third that day, and headed upstairs to face Vesta. She looked tired but not upset. He'd gotten good at reading that difference in faces.

"Oh, Romie, you just get one thing after another heaped on your shoulders. Nora Findlay came along to give me a hand soon as the ambulance pulled out. She's like as not ready to give up her apron, and you're like as not hungry enough to eat half the sandwiches we've got ready."

He would have admitted to being hungry but Vesta didn't give him a chance.

"I hadn't meant to be feeding a crowd this late, but they're lingering. Soup, sandwiches, hot coffee, hot water for tea. I've sold a good amount of wine and beer. Folks like a drink when there's been some excitement."

He saw Granny standing beside Vesta, grinning at him like she did when he'd done something that pleased her. He blinked and she was gone, replaced by Nora, who winked. He wrapped an apron around his skinny hips and grabbed a sandwich. "Ready, Coach."

"I'm glad to help," Nora said. "When it quiets down I want to show you some photos, if Tom gets them downloaded."

Vesta turned the Closed sign on at nine. Tom, who'd been sipping coffee, laid out photos of Iris lying on the beach, Earl standing there, mouth open, probably talking about suing.

"Wow," Romar said. "How'd you get those shots?"

"Nora's sneaky," Tom said. "That plus a long lens."

"These will be the insurance the guy said you'd better have," Nora said. "I didn't like his attitude, though he could have been transferring his guilt feelings into a threat to cover up his own inadequacies."

"Right, transferring," Romar said. "You talk like the school counselor I had to see after my granny died. I didn't understand her, either."

"Nora's background is in psychology," Tom said. "She's smart, not just sneaky. Good with a camera, too."

"What's this about needing insurance?" Vesta asked. "If that old codger was threatening to sue, I'll kick him out of my park the minute he gets back. I'll call Ian on his cell and tell him to let the old goat find another way back from the hospital. I'll . . ."

The door opened, setting off the chimes. "Hello, Sweetheart," Ian said, holding keys in one hand, the open door for Earl in the other. "You have any soup left? Some sandwiches? Earl here is nearly starved. Docs are keeping Iris overnight for observation."

Romar blocked them out while Tom and Nora gathered their photos and Vesta gathered her composure.

Romar said, "Soup and sandwiches coming up at Table One. Here, have a seat." He looked into Fourteen's eyes like he looked at a basketball opponent, a set grin working in his favor. Fourteen, looked down. Easy score.

"Something to drink?" Vesta asked. "Coffee or tea?"

"Decaf. A little brandy would be nice."

Ian said, "No alcoholic beverages served, but we can offer carry-out to your rig. You'll have to supply your own brandy. We can sell you beer or wine."

Earl shifted in his chair, making it groan. "Nah, I'll stay put. Get my equilibrium back, you know what I mean? Seeing Iris take a fall like that shook me up."

Earl leaned across his big belly to spoon in his soup, then leaned back to eat his sandwiches. It took three thick ham and cheese with lettuce, tomatoes and onions on sourdough to fill him. He topped them off with most of the plate of cookies Vesta set on the table.

Once the RV Park quieted down and the parking lot emptied, Romar reached Kyra for an online chat. Though he'd seen her the day before, it seemed like a month. It took her forever to respond to the Earl story. She wrote, "Mom says to stretch out on your back and line up all your crystals to get rid of the bad vibes. Luv ya, K."

Yeah, right, her standard signature. He fell asleep wondering if her mom read over her shoulder, and woke up an hour later on a bed of crystals that felt like plain old rocks. He'd dreamed that Vesta's former caretaker showed up wanting his job back. The guy in the dream looked like Earl.

Romar drank a bottle of water, cleared the crystals off the bed and opened the windows wide enough to hear the ocean. When he got upstairs the next morning, Ian was helping Vesta get ready to open. Ten minutes to go. So Ian must've spent the night. That thought pleased Romar. He whistled while he checked shelves, pulled jars and boxes to the front, noted what needed restocking.

"I don't mind being busy," Vesta said, "since customers now keep the bills paid through the winter, but I could do with less drama."

"Right, sweetheart," Ian said. "Hear that, Romar? Set a dull pace for the day and you'll see a raise in your next pay envelope."

"He hasn't had his first pay yet," Vesta said. "He needs to open a checking account."

"We'll take care of that today, once we get Iris back here with Earl and get them on their way. He'll need a cosigner, since he's a minor. You or me?"

"You," Vesta said, "since I'm his employer. I need to remember that I'm his employer, not his grandmother. I'm overworking him. Sometimes I worry I'm violating child labor laws."

"Sometimes I worry you'll worry yourself to death over this place."

Ian had Iris back with Earl before noon. Romar delivered lunch to their rig shortly after. Iris tried to give Romar twenty dollars for tending to her when she fell, but Earl stopped her.

"For Christ's sake, woman, he was doing his job, he gets paid. Your grandmother does pay you, right?"

"Vesta pays me and feeds me," he said. "Can I bring you anything else?"

"Cookies," Earl said. "You got any more of them homemade cookies? Me and Iris like a little sweet after a meal."

Vesta baked fresh cookies, muttering about being sued for diabetes next. "As of today, we're back to closing the kitchen when Millie leaves. Two in the afternoon, no exceptions, the remainder of the summer. I don't care who's starved, when the deli case is empty, that's it. Mondays and Tuesdays, when Millie's off, we just might close earlier. Romie, put yourself on a forty-hour work week and stick to it. Write your hours in my book same as Millie."

"Will do, coach," he said. As soon as he and Ian were in the car heading for the bank, he asked if Earl still threatened to sue.

"No," Ian said. "Vesta's just wearing herself out with that business, and that damn idiot Earl came in with money to pay for another five nights. Said Iris needs to rest before they move on, and he wants meals served, dinner, too, and damned if Vesta didn't agree. That's women for you. Listen to what they do more than what they say, and give them a wide berth when they're agitated. Don't bother arguing. You'll never be right and, in the rare case that you are, you'll end up losing worse than if you were wrong."

"Okay," Romar said. "You're the ref, I already know better than to argue with the ref." He glanced at the check Vesta gave him. Four hundred dollars for two weeks work less withholding required by law. She'd handed it to him in an envelope, told him she probably owed him for more hours than that so he'd have to take more beach time in the future.

"Checking account, or savings?" Ian asked. "Checking's easier when school starts and the bills roll in, but it's also easier to get at and spend. Dates and what have you."

"Yeah, right. Dates," Romar said.

"Checking for now, savings when you get your next check?" Ian asked. We'll use my address. That'll make it easier when you enroll in school. No hassle over Vesta's place being over the county line. And, by the way, use my address when you correspond with your mother. Or

Salty's. No need to have Vesta's address floating around inside a prison."

He hadn't thought about that worry. He looked out the window. "One more thing and I'll foul out."

"How's that?" Ian had slowed to wait for passing cars before pulling into a parking lot.

"The worries I've brought Vesta. I lied about my age, I got Earl threatening a lawsuit, she's worried about child labor laws, she needs to worry about my prisoner mother knowing her address. That's four fouls."

Ian parked the car, turned off the key and put a hand on Romar's arm. "Okay, listen up. You're the best thing that's happened to Vesta in a very long time. Best thing for the Jarvi clan, too. Might as well use Salty's address since she's already written to your mother."

They opened a checking account with Romar's pay, a savings account with the one hundred dollars he still had that came from his granny. "Anything you need before we head back?" Ian asked when they were back in the car.

"Official picture ID. And a decent basketball. I'm giving Amber and Jade lessons."

"Good," Ian said. "While you're at it, give them lessons on running a vacuum cleaner or sweeping the floor once in awhile. Leila spoils them. Vesta frets over that, too. Kyra's her favorite, hands down."

Romar wanted to say he knew the feeling, but they'd already stopped at Yachats Mercantile, where he bought a good ball and a hand pump.

That evening, when things were quiet, he practiced dribbling on Vesta's parking lot and made mock passes to get his shoulders and arms into shape. "Getting ready for the twins' lesson," he told Vesta.

"There must be somewhere you can hang a basket, Romie. Maybe the end of the shelter. Or above the laundry room door."

"Nah," he said. "When the ball hits the building, it jars everything. Aunt Joan couldn't stand it when I had a hoop on the garage. 'Sides, it left smudges on the paint."

#

When he saw Kyra on Wednesday, she'd finished only one algebra problem and he'd written only one line to his mother. "Here's an idea," she said. "You do my algebra lessons online like its one of your classes, and I'll write your letter."

Amber had grabbed the new ball when he walked in the door. She bounced it on the kitchen floor while Jade bounced herself and said, "How're my moves, Romar?" Or maybe Jade had the ball and Amber the moves.

Romar grabbed the ball midbounce, his eyes squinted to study Kyra's face. "You're joking, right? I mean, you wouldn't cheat to get through algebra."

She shrugged. "I guess I'd rather fail than have some guy do my work. Even a sort of relative guy."

"She hates the teacher," Jade said.

"Nunh uh," Amber said. "She hates Bruno Muscle Man."

"Who used to be her boyfriend. And you're s'posed to call him Bradley Mustanen. Mom said."

"See why I don't have time to study? I've got the twins twenty-four seven."

"Nunh uh, only sixteen seven," Amber said.

Jade added, "'cause we sleep eight hours."

"Except when I'm helping Mom with her cottage-cleaning contract. Salty watches them then. Plus, Mom's got me making crystal pendants for the Fourth of July . . . the busiest day of the year in Yachats.

"You can give us a basketball lesson."

"While Kyra works on algebra."

"Deal," Romar said. "Go outside, do some warm-up stretches, run around Salty's cottage twice, I'll get Kyra started on a problem."

The twins bumped their way through the door, letting the screen slap shut behind them.

"So," Romar said, his eyes watching Kyra's, "tell me about this Bradley guy that used to be your boyfriend."

"He was never my boyfriend. He's a creep who sat behind me in algebra and blew on my hair. Stupid stuff like that. I dropped out because the teacher wouldn't let me move to another seat."

Romar snickered in a way that let Kyra know he didn't believe she'd dropped out because a teacher wouldn't let her change seats.

Kyra's eyes went hard as her mother's crystals. "That's all there is to tell."

She'd pressed her lips together and poked out her chin. She reminded him of Granny. Or of Vesta when she announced they would stick to their two o'clock restaurant closing. He remembered what Ian said about arguing with women.

"Okay," he said, "I'll go shoot some hoop with the twins."

He'd give her some time, come at the Bradley question another way, find out what the guy did besides blowing on her hair.

Kyra came out an hour later. "I did a chapter for you to check, Salty's coming over with a piece of paper so you can write your letter, and the twins can keep practicing or go to their rooms."

"Practicing," they said. "Drive the key. Block out. Take your shot. Watch us, Kyra."

Salty arrived with a letter written out for him to copy. She was dressed like she'd been the first time he met her.

"I've been thinking about this matter," she whispered. The bright scarf she'd tied around her head tickled his arm. "Don't tell your mother too much, just that you have a summer job and that you're starting a new school in the fall. I talked to Vesta and Ian both. We all agreed. That's based on things Vesta's heard about people in prison or jail. They all want money."

"Does she have legal rights to money I earn?" Romar whispered back, the sweat on his body going cold.

"No, not according to Ian. It's just that you might feel sorry for her, being inside for so long and all."

"I'm kinda hoping she feels sorry for me, leaving like she did."

Salty glanced at Kyra coming through the door. "Time will tell."

"Tell what?" Kyra asked.

"Oh, this and that about his mother. If he looks like her and what have you. I think we should go up to Washington before the end of July. There's the Holistic Health Fair the first weekend in August . . . that's always big for crystal sales. Then all sorts of school stuff starts. What do you think, Kyra?"

"I think Mom's going to pitch a fit when I ask to go along."

"Do you mind if she rides along, Romar?" Salty asked. "She can't go inside the prison with us, but she can see some scenery along the way. She's almost sixteen. It's time she had a trip somewhere."

Romar shrugged. "I might get a little uptight, not be my usual charming self. You know, facing a new opponent on an unknown court and all." He was already uptight, but right now Salty was calling the plays.

19

FIREWORKS

Romar's letter to his mother sounded about right.

Dear Mother, I'm looking forward to meeting you. Salena Jarvi, who remembers Granny from when they were girls, is making the arrangements. I met her through my summer job.

Yours truly, Romar Andrew Jones

Salena said "Yours truly" worked just fine when you didn't know someone personally, even when it's your mother. He didn't want to write "Love, Romar" since that wouldn't be true. You couldn't love someone you didn't know. He loved Granny and his dad, but he wouldn't be writing them letters. He liked Vesta well enough to sign a letter with "Love" if he needed to write to her. He already signed e-mails to Kyra just like she did. Luv ya. It didn't mean anything.

Vesta's RV park filled up on Friday, half emptied on Sunday and filled again Tuesday, the night before the fourth of July.

"No algebra lesson on the 4th," Kyra wrote. "Yachats rocks all day and Vesta's will be busy, 'specially if the weather's good. Course I'll be herding the twins while Mom works. Everybody hangs at the state park at the river. Fireworks there at dark. Look for me in the main parking lot around six if you can get Auntie Gram to close on time. If you can't make it, call me on my friend Emily's cell."

She gave him a number he memorized. Numbers were easy. He caught a ride from Vesta's that got him to Yachats in time to check out things for sale in booths and shops. Nothing he needed. Except food.

Waves crashed on rocks along the town shore, then settled to roll in over the broad sand beach at the river mouth. It looked like it had been swept for the party. Swept and washed by waves that climbed the backs of those ahead and rode into the river. There had to be a poem in there somewhere, but he'd need time and quiet to write one.

He smelled pizza and thought about digging out his money when he heard Kyra call his name. She ran to meet him, gave him a quick hug and grabbed another girl's hand. Both had on open white blouses over tank tops that showed off their figures. Romar knew girls liked guys to notice, but he hadn't figured out how to say they looked good before Kyra was talking.

"This is Emily, she lives in Waldport. And this is Romar."

Emily had long straight hair, too, darker than Kyra's. Her eyes reminded him of his own – a light brown color. "Hi, Romar. You're even cuter than Kyra said."

A swarm of girls surrounded them, all talking at once, one grabbing his left hand, another rubbing his right arm. He should have carried a basketball to bounce. It would give him something to do when he couldn't find anything to say.

"Hey," Kyra said, "he's taken. Hands off."

The dark-haired girl who still held his hand said, "No way, Kyra. You said he's your cousin." She lifted his hand to her lips. "I'm Roz Ryan, I'm a cheerleader, Kyra says you'll be on our basketball team next year."

"Yeah, maybe," Romar said, his eyes on Kyra, begging for help. Five girls, maybe six, circling around might be a guy's dream, but he didn't know how to handle it. He felt boxed in like two seven-foot-tall guys were blocking him. He couldn't make his mouth form words or his feet move.

Kyra was busy explaining the cousin thing that made them related but distant, when a guy gang moved in on them. Probably following the girl swarm.

One no-neck guy with rounded shoulders and a soft belly turned out to be Bradley Mustanen, though Romar didn't learn that fact until later. No Neck maneuvered his way behind Kyra, got too close to her and planted his hands on her biceps. He squeezed so hard his knuckles went white.

Kyra grimaced. "Ouch, Bradley, let go." Her eyes glistened. One tear escaped and ran down her cheek.

Romar felt the adrenaline rush he got when tension mounted in a game. He needed to shed the girls who had him trapped and put the Bradley guy in check.

Bradley lifted Kyra off her feet.

Time to take his shot. Romar twisted left, then right. The girls backed up. He reached over Kyra and karate chopped the spot where Brad's head rested on his body. *Left side, go for the nerve.* His dad's voice calling the play.

Bradley grunted. His breath reeked of stale beer. His left hand opened; his right stayed locked on Kyra's arm.

Romar moved to position himself so he could use his right hand on the other side of Bradley's neck. In the split second that repositioning took, a kid with curly black hair got in the way.

"Hey!" Romar said.

The kid held something at Bradley's neck. Switchblade? Stiletto? Nail file?

"Let go of the lady's arm, Bradley, my man. Men don't treat women like that, least not where I come from."

When Bradley's hand relaxed, his buddies pulled him away from Kyra. Romar moved her toward Emily and the other girls, meaning to go after Bradley, but the curly-haired kid was in his face, grinning, both hands out and open. No knife.

"Carlos Martinez, Esquire," the kid said. "We're cool. We're not looking for trouble, just chatting up the girls, you know what I'm saying? You take care of your girl and I'll take care of the bulldog."

Tears ran down Kyra's cheeks. Romar swiped one side of her face with his fingers, focused on Bradley, trying to keep Carlos in his line of vision, too. "I'm Romar Jones, Kyra's my cousin, you put your hands on her again I'll rip off your head."

One of the guys who had a hand on Bradley's arm said, "Hey, we're out of here, man."

Romar heard Kyra sniffing and Emily comforting her. Maybe all the girls comforting. He kept his eyes on Bradley and the gang. They left without Carlos.

"I'll be going, too, Romar Jones," Carlos said, big grin showing nice teeth. "Catch you later."

"Who was that Mexican guy?" Roz asked.

"I don't know," Emily said, "but he's cute. Curls and dimples."

"Yeah, and a knife," Roz said.

Kyra sniffed. "Are you sure, Roz? I think he just had sharp fingernails."

Roz groaned. "Right, sharp fingernails will stop the Brad type every time."

The kid had a small knife. Romar was with Roz on that, but he stayed out of the girls' conversation. A small knife and quick moves could be good on the basketball court. Any sport for that matter.

A woman walked up to the girls like she wanted to join them for a chat. "Hello," she said, her eyes touching each of them. When she got to Romar, her eyes settled for a second too long, telegraphing her next move. Referee, stepping into the game.

"Kyra, are you okay?"

"I'm fine, Ms. Sullivan," Kyra said. "This is my cousin, Romar Jones. He's living out here, he'll be at Waldport when school starts."

"Aleta Sullivan." The woman extended a hand to Romar.

He gave her hand a firm shake, careful not to squeeze too hard. She had soft skin. Heat climbed up his chest and neck. What was that about?

The woman turned back to Kyra. "Let me have a look at your arms. I saw Bradley grab you. I saw the whole group earlier. They've been drinking, but they didn't have anything visible, and it's never a good idea for a teacher to step into that kind of situation."

Kyra shrugged her shoulders so the blouse slid down around her elbows. So, she trusted the teacher. Both of Kyra's arms had deep red spots where Bradley's fingers pressed into her flesh. Romar wanted to kiss the spots like his granny kissed his hurts when he was little. And he wanted to track Bradley, get him alone, take him down.

Ms. Sullivan frowned. "I think you need to ice those. There's a first aid booth out by the highway. You should report Bradley."

Right. Ice, not kisses. Romar touched Kyra's back, just to remind her he was still there.

"I'm okay," Kyra said. Tears started again. "Reporting will just make things worse. Besides, Romar karate chopped Bradley."

"And the other kid . . ."

"Shh!"

"What other kid?" Ms. Sullivan asked.

"One of their group stepped in," Romar said. "Subdued Bradley just like that." He snapped his fingers. He wasn't certain who'd mentioned the other kid, or who said "shh," but he wanted it dropped.

Ms. Sullivan gave him the look all teachers use to let you know they know what you're up to, but they'll wait for you to trip up. "What year are you, Romar?"

"Uh, sophomore. If I can get in. I have to finish my freshman year. The last two weeks and finals."

"You'll get in," she said, that look still in place. "It's a public school."

"He needs someone to monitor his finals," Kyra said.

"The school administration can help with that. Have your former school contact our office."

"Ms. Sullivan teaches English and drama," Kyra said, glancing at Romar, then back at Ms. Sullivan. "He's caretaker at Vesta's By the Sea right now, so it would help if he could take the tests at the Yachats' library. You know, not try to get to Waldport."

A frown crossed Ms. Sullivan's face. "Vesta's is in Lane County."

"But his official address is in Waldport."

"Ah, good."

"Kyra's my personal representative," Romar said. He gave Ms. Sullivan, English teacher, his best smile, wondering if she'd have a conversation about him with Mr. Whitley.

"And Romar's tutoring me in algebra. It sort of evens out."

The whole group trekked to the fire department booth, where a paramedic examined Kyra's bruises while Ms. Sullivan and six girls explained the incident. The paramedic activated two instant cold packs and talked about deep tissue bruising. He had Kyra flex her arm. She winced, but she had decent biceps. She could defend herself if Bradley came at her face to face. But she needed to tell the truth about the guy. He'd done a lot more than blow her hair to make her drop out of algebra. Romar knew that much.

Six girl voices plus one woman's voice kept Romar's head rotating until he felt dizzy. Roz had a vice grip hold on his hand. He heard "Good job," felt pats on his back. He'd scored with the girls, but the game wasn't over.

Romar's mind pictures of cuddling with Kyra on a blanket on the beach were nothing like the reality when they watched fireworks over Yachats' Bay. They cuddled, sort of, and they had a blanket. They also had Kyra's mother and the twins, Salena, Vesta and Ian, Emily and Roz. And Carlos, who'd come up alongside him while the girls were staking out their place to sit.

"Romar, how's your girl? Those firefighter guys take good care of her?"

Romar studied the kid. For some reason he liked what he saw. "Carlos, you packing a knife?"

"No way," Carlos said, his voice so melodic the two words sounded like a song. He patted his jeans, front and back, to show there were no protrusions.

"What about your socks? They empty, too"

"You carry your knife in your socks?" Carlos asked.

"Nah," Romar said. "Mine's a skinning knife. I wear it out in the open, on my hip. Skin cougars alive when they dare to come at me."

Carlos laughed and held up his right hand. "Hey, you got more girls than you can take care of, right?"

Romar grabbed the offered hand, the one that had held something at Bradley's neck. "Maybe."

"Want to invite me to join you?"

"You sure you're ready?" Romar pointed to the group of women and girls watching them.

"Oh, man," Carlos said. He settled between Emily and Roz, but not until he'd met all the others, repeated their names and asked if they were comfortable.

The adults heard three versions of the Bradley encounter, including Carlos's role. They fussed over Kyra's bruised arms. Kyra squeezed Romar's hand, leaned into him, and gave him a nice goodnight kiss with a touch of tongue. He grinned all the way back to Vesta's.

He slept well that night and wakened with the saying, *"He who fights and runs away will live to fight another day,"* playing in his head. One of the sayings Whitley made them analyze, not so much for meaning but for accuracy of origin. Sayings attributed to someone's spoken rather than written words. Sort of like Whitley was there reminding him Bradley would be back.

Another thought grabbed him while sleep lingered: he liked Mr. Whitley.

20

SUMMER STORM

By mid-July Romar had completed his assignments online. Ms. Sullivan monitored his final tests at the Yachats library. Far as Romar knew, she hadn't spoken with any of his Roseburg teachers. He sent Mr. Whitley the poem that he started writing in his head when he reached the dunes, rewritten in present tense. He hoped it would make the grade – a good grade that would impress his new school when they looked at his transcript.

Sun glistens on waves washing the shore
Blowing sand stings a bearded face
Sand in shoes   biting
Sand on legs
Static cling

Whitely sent back a note saying that Romar owed him one more poem for ditching detention the day he walked out of school. An explanation for his behavior. He began composing: *My mother's in prison, my dad and Granny are dead . . .* but he wasn't ready to go there. Not before he met his mother.

On his Wednesday trips to Yachats to help Kyra with algebra and the twins with basketball, he kept an eye out for Carlos. He wouldn't mind getting to know some guys his age. According to Kyra, Emily and Roz were both trying to find out more about the guy they called the cute Mexican, but nobody knew anything. They decided he must have been a tourist.

Romar tried to get more information about Bradley, prepare himself for what might happen when school started. Kyra shrugged off his prying, saying only that she didn't appreciate Bradley's unwelcome attention, so she dropped the only class they shared.

He let it go. They spent some time studying the website of the prison where his mother lived. It showed the prison visiting room, plus information about Gig Harbor and area motels.

Later, back in his caretaker's room, Romar read everything he could find online about drug-related crimes . . . possession, manufacture, delivery. He figured out a few things. Possession with intent to deliver was more serious than possession with intent to use. Even possession of ingredients to make meth could get a person a prison sentence.

"Meth . . . Society's Menace," one headline read. He looked at pictures of users who went from young and attractive to old and haggard in a matter of weeks on the drug. He tried to picture his mother, but the only clue he had came from Aunt Joan. "You got those weak eyes from your mother."

On an evening beach run, he watched clouds forming on the horizon, white at first, darkening in minutes, moving fast. They blocked the sun. Wind kicked up, cooled the sweat on his chest and back, bringing shivers. He felt Granny beside him. *Put on your shirt, Romie. Turn back now. Summer storms on the ocean can carry lightning.*

Fat raindrops fell with such force they left divots in the sand. Thunder began like a distant drum, growing closer, louder. He picked up the pace, aided by wind blowing in from the sea.

There were a dozen RVs in Vesta's park, some of them with older owners. None as out of shape as Earl and Iris, but a few who would need help with awnings.

A flash lit the darkening sky for a long second when he reached the stairs. A folding lawn chair flew past. He retrieved it and another, abandoned by their owners. He secured them in the shelter and went through the RV Park to make sure all awnings were in and all guests prepared if the power went out.

"No matter the task, you know how to handle it," Vesta said, pulling him in and locking .the door.

"Granny and my dad both taught me stuff you don't learn in school. Like what you heard about me trying to get the Bradley guy's hands off Kyra. My dad told me it's better to stun a guy for a few seconds with a chop than with a fist. I practiced on a big old stuffed bear he'd won for me at a carnival."

He couldn't get Bradley off his mind.

"Bradley's a bully," Vesta said, and patted his arm, a gesture he'd come to expect. "You had a good start in life. Maybe he didn't. Well, we're buttoned up here. The storm should blow over soon, but I'll sleep with both ears open. You take a spare flashlight downstairs, just in case."

Romar fell asleep to hard rain and pounding surf, and wakened from a dream back in the Glide house with Granny and his dad. He'd been young, frightened by night noises that Granny said were trees talking back to the wind. His dad promised to trim branches that tapped his window.

It took almost a minute to get his head and body together and into the present. He looked for the clock or the light on the small microwave. Nothing. Power out.

The noise he'd heard in his dream started up again, tap tap tap. No trees touched his room windows or any part of the building. He grabbed his jeans, pulled them on both legs at once, used his feet to search for shoes and get them on.

He lifted the blind away from the window. Rain fell, a soft rain without wind. Absolute silence, then tap tap tap. The sound came from beyond the wall. The furnace? Power outage must have done something to the furnace.

He groped in the dark, found the flashlight, took time to think. The furnace ran on propane with an electric igniter. They'd had a similar setup in Glide. Without power there couldn't be any sound. Unless something went wrong in the gas line.

He heard the sound again . . . tap . . . tap . . . tap. Not as close together as it was the first time he heard it. Could be the dungeon room door. Maybe he'd forgotten to close and lock it when he left Vesta. His mind had been on Kyra, wondering if thunder and lightning scared her like it did some people.

The flashlight's beam startled him, though he'd turned it on. He switched it off. The rhythm changed to tap . . . tap . . . click. Too steady for a door. Someone was in the dungeon room.

He swept his hand over the wall by the door for the keys and sorted them by feel – laundry room key longer than dungeon key. He reached for the door handle.

Click . . . clunk. He backed away from the door, slid open the drawer where he kept his dad's knife hidden under clean socks and underwear.

Be prepared.

His dad's voice, with Granny chiming in.

Think first. Trust your instincts.

He lifted the phone from its cradle. Dead.

He unlocked his room door, eased it open, slipped through into the dark wet night and counted to twenty. No sound, not even rain, though his arms already felt wet.

He crept along the building wall to the laundry room door and pushed against it enough to know it wasn't locked. He pushed again, heard the hinges squeak, counted to thirty. Nothing.

He took the knife from its sheath, held it in his right hand, the flashlight in his left and kicked the door open. Still nothing. He planted his feet for balance, a quick pivot if need be, waiting for his eyes to adjust to the dark. Washer lids up like he left them. Dryers closed. Dungeon room door closed.

He pocketed the unlit flashlight, kept the knife ready in his right hand and crept along the cement floor. Reached the dungeon room door, jerked it open, used it as a shield.

Saw a sliver of light that lasted two heartbeats and went out. Heard a gasp, followed by the thunk and clatter of a tool hitting the door and landing on the floor.

He shifted his weight to his back foot, steadied the knife, grabbed the flash and aimed the light toward the stench that filled his nostrils.

"Meth Mouth," he said to the scruffy beard and blinking eyes. "Dalton, right?"

One door of the locked metal cabinet angled out at the bottom. Tools littered the floor. Romar held the knife pointed at Dalton's throat, blocked with his left arm when Dalton made a move, let out a howl meant to sound like a wounded coyote. It came out a Tarzan imitation, like the cartoon Tarzan sounded. He took a breath, let loose again, grabbing Dalton's wrist and twisting. "I'll stick this knife in you if you try to run."

The man's wrist and arm had no substance. His rancid breath came out in sobs that turned to heaves. He fell to his knees, retching. Romar kept a tight hold on the frail wrist, wondering if he was breaking or crushing the bones.

Vesta's emergency air horn, that odd gift Ian had given her one Christmas, pierced the night. She'd heard Dalton, too. Or the Tarzan imitation. Everyone in the RV Park would hear that horn.

Dalton sobbed. The air reeked of rotten breath and urine. Maybe fear, too.

Footfalls moving fast down the stairs. Silence. Another flashlight beam cutting the darkness. "Romie? Oh, dear God, it's Dalton."

"I called nine-one-one on my cell," a deep voice said from the black night. "Figured there's no track and field events going on out here. I've got a gun. Loaded."

Dalton heaved. Spittle dripped from his mouth, tears from his eyes.

Anger drained out of Romar. His stomach churned. He wanted his granny in case he puked, too. She'd always been there to wash his face and clean him up.

"His name's Dalton, he needs juice, something with sugar," Vesta said to the deep voice. "I'm going upstairs to get him something. Don't shoot him unless he makes a move toward my grandson."

The red and blue lights rotating in the mist looked like Vesta's by the Sea had a private fireworks show. It went on long past dawn, though one police car with two officers had taken Dalton away. Romar stood watch while one policeman cuffed and shackled him.

Had policemen done that to his mother? Had she cried? Wet herself like Dalton did? Begged for something to stop the tremors?

The remaining officers took photos of the laundry room and dungeon. They went through the metal cabinet, the one Vesta called the chemical cupboard, listing every item. Paint cans stacked up in one area, flammable cleaners in another.

It didn't take an Einstein to figure out they were only interested in the cache on the bottom shelf: three plastic-wrapped boxes filled with cold tablet packets, twenty one-ounce bottles of iodine, and a shoebox with assorted brown prescription bottles.

They'd found two keys on Dalton, one to the laundry room, the other to the dungeon. That interested them too.

"My husband locked up anything he considered flammable or poisonous," Vesta said, when they asked about the muriatic acid and lye. "He died eight years ago."

Romar figured Vesta's eyes might burn a hole in the questioner's shirt.

"Like I already said, Dalton only had the key to that cabinet one time. He was looking for paint to do some touch-up. I got the key back from him the same day, after he'd finished painting. He wasn't much good at it, he left paint drips everywhere."

"What about these?" An officer held a Sterno can in each hand.

"For all I know they could be left over from the war. Never in life have I cooked anything in small enough quantity to fit over one of those little cans."

"How did Dalton Grimes come by the door keys?"

"Since they're copies, I'm guessing you can figure that out. He kept a set in the caretaker's room. He used my car about once a week to run errands, so he had plenty of opportunity to get copies."

"You ever see anyone hanging around him? Someone who wasn't one of your typical guests or customers?"

Vesta drilled them with her sharp eyes one more time. "When you run a business on a highway like this one, five miles or so from the closest town, you see every kind of human life that ever walked. You make mental notes from the moment the door opens. Before, even. The moment a vehicle pulls off the road. Now and again you'll have a customer who drops something in his pocket, and you let it go. You pick your battles."

"Anyone stop by on a regular basis who might have been supplying Grimes?"

She intensified her look. "No."

"Just 'No'? No other comment?"

"Look, I've told you Dalton used my car for errands. Personal errands along with picking up things for me. He had a good thing going here. Room and board, decent wages. I'm guessing he would do illegal business away from my place. And, I'm guessing the items you found in that locker came onto the premises here not long before that night he took off with my car. I'm guessing he needed a fix right then."

"Okay, that's it for now."

When the officers left, Vesta had a receipt for items taken from the cabinet and Romar a receipt for his dad's knife. They both had dry throats from answering the same questions asked ten different ways.

Vesta turned on a couple emergency lights, set one soup pot brewing what she called pot coffee on the stove, another heating soup. She tried to smile, but her eyes stayed as misty as the weather.

"Soup's an odd breakfast but folks need something hot to settle their stomachs. Lucky for them I cook with propane, not electricity."

Romar tried to smile back. "It's getting late enough to call it lunch. What else are we serving? Crackers and cheese? Juice and candy bars?"

He had another thought. "How'd you know to get juice into Dalton? You been around druggies?"

"Dalton started going through a lot of juice last summer. I wouldn't have kept track if it hadn't been unusual. Ian had suspicions about Dalton even before the juice and candy thing, but I pooh-poohed it."

"So, did Ian suspect it was meth?"

"Ian thought cocaine. He went through the caretaker's room, the dungeon and the laundry room one day when Dalton was off running errands. None of that stuff was on the premises at the time, Ian will tell you that. I'm guessing Dalton stashed it just before Labor Day weekend."

Romar nodded. "And then needed something to hold him over until the person cooking came along with money for the stuff he'd stashed."

"That would be my guess," Vesta said.

A second or two later, she whacked the counter with a big spoon. Soup droplets flew into the air. "Romie, you should not have tried to handle Dalton by yourself,"

"I know. You already said, but I knew what I'd find before I opened the dungeon room door. It seemed like I didn't do it alone. It seemed like it needed to get settled. I couldn't let him get away again."

Vesta shook her head, then wrapped her arms around his waist. "Did you mind that I called you my grandson?"

He rested his chin on her head and hugged her shoulders. "Nah, you're my second grandma. It's okay to have two."

21

VISITING DAY

A week later a detective returned Vesta's old chemicals and Romar's dad's knife. Dalton's stashed pills and iodine cleared up a drugstore theft in Florence, but police were still looking for the meth manufacturer. They figured Dalton Grimes had a contact supplying him, likely not far from where they'd found him and Vesta's car the summer before. This time he'd go to prison, not an honor camp.

They said they had no idea if Dalton had camped on the beach or in the wilderness to be near Vesta's. That didn't jibe with what Ian heard from his forest service contacts, who figured it was Dalton, and that he was cooking something on a camp stove to tide him over. Serious meth labs wouldn't set up so close to civilization.

"Finally, the end to our roles in a bad movie," Vesta said. "We can put this whole mess behind us and plan your trip to meet your mother."

They left at nine the last Friday morning in July, Salena driving, Kyra navigating. Vesta sent them with coolers full of food and drinks and a big thermos of coffee. Ian handed them a cell phone with instructions to keep Vesta posted.

Romar settled in the backseat of Salena's Corolla with his notebook computer open, ready to record their journey. Waldport, where he might live during the coming school year. Newport, where the Matlocks stayed but didn't invest. Depoe Bay, with its seawall on one side of the highway and a long stretch of shops on the other.

Lincoln City, with seven miles of beaches and an outlet center where Salena and Kyra hoped to shop on their way back home.

They took the Portland cutoff north of Lincoln City, stopped at a day park for a picnic that Romar managed to eat in spite of a churning stomach. Pre-game nerves. Eat light, drink lots of water. The cutoff joined Interstate 5 about one hundred seventy-five miles north of where he'd walked under it exactly eight weeks earlier.

"I'd forgotten how many lanes they have on these freeways," Salena said. "It's a straight shot into Washington now. I'd appreciate it if no one talks."

Romar nodded, in case she looked in the rear view mirror. Salena gripped the steering wheel at ten and two o'clock, and leaned forward like that would help her see around cars and trucks whizzing past them. No one said a word until they saw the 'Welcome to Washington' sign on the bridge across the Columbia River.

"We're in Washington," Kyra said. "My first time out of Oregon."

"Well, don't step out of the car yet," Salena said. "We're right above a mighty big river. They wrote a song about it." She sang "*Roll on Columbia, Roll on.*"

Kyra laughed until she got hiccups. That made him laugh until tears leaked out of his eyes. More pre-game nerves for certain.

They pulled into a motel a few miles west of the prison a little before five. Romar's debit card went through with no problem. Something over one hundred dollars deducted from his account. Twice that if they stayed a second night. He'd done the math before they left; he'd have enough for meals, lodging and gas. He needed to pay for this trip.

Their suite had a bedroom for Salena and Kyra, a hide-a-bed in the main room for him, a small kitchen where they could fix breakfast. If any of them felt like eating. The whole set-up good enough for their needs.

They got back in the car to make a test drive by the prison. It took a car honking behind them to get Salena into a roundabout at the prison exit. She'd hushed them again. Romar and Kyra both offered to drive. Salena shook her head. "Neither one of you have a driver's license. We're near a prison. I let either of you drive, I'm the one they'll lock up."

"I've got a learner's permit," Kyra said.

"Hush about driving," Salena said.

"Seventy-five acres, all fenced in," Romar read on the computer printout he'd brought.

"It doesn't look like such a bad place," Kyra said.

"Except for the fences and razor wire." He pictured a woman who could be his mother standing at the fence, looking for a way out.

They turned around in the parking lot and followed directions the motel clerk had given them to reach Gig Harbor's waterfront. Salena let out a high whining sound when she drove back through the round-about and discovered she had to get into and out of one more.

They found the view of Mount Rainier and fishing boats and yachts shown on the town's official web site and chose a Mexican restaurant across from one of the marinas. Romar got out his debit card, but Salena said, "This is on Ian. He gave me money for meals out, and you're not to argue. Now, we'll walk a ways to let our food settle."

"Little as Romar ate, he'll only need to walk a block," Kyra said. She took his hand and held it, squeezing every now and then. "I know it's hard."

Salena walked in front of them, her boots with crystals on them clicking with each step, a bright pink jacket over black top and pants, and crystal earrings that dangled to her shoulders.

In the morning they left Kyra in the motel with coffee, orange juice and cinnamon rolls. She cried when she gave Romar a little good-luck kiss. That about undid him. He stared out the passenger window of Salena's car until they reached the prison parking lot.

The building looked like it had online – a covered entrance angled in between two buildings. They got there at ten for ten-thirty visiting, waited outside until someone led the group in and lined up at the check-in desk. Salena put her purse in a locker. She wore all black, including flat black shoes, and no crystals. No jewelry except for a gold wedding band.

Romar wore a white dress shirt Ian gave him and clean jeans. He'd intended to wear a pair of khaki pants, the only decent pair he brought from Roseburg, but they didn't reach his ankles. He should have known. The last time he had them on was for Granny's funeral.

He shook his hands like he was loosening up for a game. He'd thought about poking a calming crystal into his pocket, but that might have gotten him sent away. Anxiety and too many people had him sweating like the final minutes in a seesaw game. He hoped his deodorant didn't fail before he got to meet his mother. The rules said they could hug when they greeted each other. He wondered if she'd expect a hug. He'd hang back, let her make the first move.

An officer in a navy blue uniform said, "This way," and led them to a table with three folding chairs. A woman with brown hair and brown glasses stood, smiling. She was about a foot shorter than him. Romar tried to smile, but it wasn't happening. Salena took over.

"Marlene Jones?" Salena asked. "I'm Salena Jarvi. Edmund Jarvi was my husband."

They were close enough for Romar to see the woman's name and picture on her badge. She looked better in person than in the picture. He watched her eyes. Nothing in them changed while Salena spoke.

"I'm Romar Andrew Jones," he said. "You must be my mother."

Marlene Jones said, "Oh, baby."

He pushed up his glasses and squinted, his old habit at work. "Um, since I'm not a baby you should probably use my name." Bzzzt, rudeness foul on him. Still nothing going on with Marlene's eyes. They sat down, Romar and Salena on one side of the table, Marlene across from them.

The visiting room filled. The inmates all wore khaki pants and shirts. Most of them had their shirts open over plain white tees. They all wore horizontal badges with their photos.

Officers wore vertical badges with their photos. They looked better in person too. Visitors' badges were plain.

Some little kids clung to women. Their mothers he guessed. Others escaped to a glassed-in children's room with Disney characters painted on the walls, smaller tables and chairs, and bins filled with toys.

"Well, start by telling me about yourself. Your letter didn't say much except that you had a summer job, and that Mrs. Jarvi is related to your dad's mother."

To my granny, he wanted to say. He squinted again so he could get a good look at his mother's eyes. They were like his, or his like hers, light brown. But hers seemed empty, almost like a blind person's would look.

"Okay, I'm fifteen and a half, I walked out of school and left Uncle Sherman and Aunt Joan's place on June first. I meant to hike all the way here to meet you, but first I had to keep a promise to Granny to take some of her ashes to Yachats. I found a job along the way. Since then, I've finished my classes . . . you can do that online these days . . . so I'll be in tenth grade when school starts."

"You're so tall, like your dad."

"Yeah, I'm starting to look like he did in some of his pictures. So, now it's your turn. You can tell me how you got here, stuff like that." He glanced at Salena, her back tight against the chair, out of the conversation.

"I knew you'd ask. All I'm going to tell you is that it's drug related. I got addicted when I was young. It's like an illness. Can you understand that?"

"Are you doing time for possession? Or transporting? Or manufacturing meth? Or something worse?"

The woman who he would have to accept was his mother leaned back, her right hand over her heart, her eyes narrowed. "How do you know those words? Those are legal words. Have you done time?"

"Nope, I'm an athlete, I don't use. And I have access to the Internet. I looked up crime classifications."

"Oh." She looked at her hands, picked a hangnail, looked up. "Well, you can tell me about that. Using the Internet. We don't have such privileges in here."

"Okay, soon as you tell me about your crime and how much time you've done and how much time you've got left."

Her eyes filled with tears. "Is that what you came here to do? To ask me questions like that?"

Tears. So, she did feel something. "Not exactly. I really came to find out why you left me when I was a baby and never came back to find me. I wrote letters asking all sorts of questions, but we never had an address so I couldn't send them."

She whispered, "What were some of the other questions?"

"They all came down to the same thing. I need to know why you left me."

"Like I said, I'm an addict. It's not really my fault, I was born to an addicted mother."

"Did she abandon you?"

His mother gasped. "I didn't abandon you, Romar. You had your father and your grandmother. She didn't like me from the get-go, and I couldn't stand living in Glide."

"Why?"

"There was nothing to do there. Your dad went off on his hikes and fishing trips, and I was stuck . . ." Her hand flew to her mouth.

"With me? You were stuck with me?"

"No, that's not what I was going to say. I was stuck in that little house with your grandmother. She made it hard for me. Try to understand what it was like. I wasn't much older than you are now when you were born."

"Yeah, Granny told me you were young, and that it was hard for you. I got that, I just don't get a mother going off and never coming back or calling or writing a letter."

"You have to understand what it's like when you have an addiction."

He heaved a sigh. Anger wasn't getting him anywhere. He hadn't expected to feel so mad at her when he saw her, but there it was.

"Okay, you're an addict, you needed to be where you could feed your habit, you did some time in Oregon. Aunt Joan told me that. You might be pleased to know that Dad never said anything negative about you. By the way, he was young, too. I just figured that out awhile ago. Anyway, he'd say, 'I'm not going to repeat negative things I've heard about your mother.' We all had a good life, Dad and Granny and me, until he was killed."

The woman he would forever after think of as Marlene rubbed away blood where she'd picked at her finger. "Tell me about your dad. Did he ever have a . . . a girlfriend?"

"Nope."

"So, what happened to his estate? When he died? Did you, like, inherit? Or did your grandmother?"

Salena dragged her chair close to the table and leaned toward Marlene. "What are you asking?"

"Well, I am the widow, though I've never done anything about it."

"You and Dad were divorced long before he was killed."

"That's not true. I never signed any papers."

"A divorce was granted when I was eight or nine. There are papers. They're in Dad's backpack."

Marlene said, "Oh," and looked past him. When she made eye contact again, she said, "I'm truly sorry about your dad and your granny. I'm sorry you got stuck with your Uncle Sherman and Aunt Joan."

Her eyes went back to her hands. "My crime has to do with manufacturing meth. I didn't do it, the manufacturing, but I lived at the place where it was being done. I got eight years, I've got five left."

The truth helped. Sorry helped. But her eyes stayed flat. She wasn't a challenging opponent.

"Okay, you've been in for three this time. Since I was twelve. A year before Dad was killed. You weren't in prison most of those twelve years, right?"

"Right."

"Where were you when you weren't in prison?"

"I moved here, to Washington. To Cathlamet, it's on the Columbia River."

Romar looked at Salena to see if she'd sing '*Roll on Columbia*', but she just sat there with her eyes narrowed.

Marlene said, "That's where the trouble started. Near there." She reached one hand part way across the table and pulled it back. "Do you think you can forgive me? I'd like to be in touch with you from now on."

He kept his hands in his lap. "I don't think I'll ever understand. I'm going on with my life, but it seems like I should know something about you."

"And I want to know all about you. Tell me more about your job, where you live, the athletic things. You know."

He pictured Vesta's, his room, the ocean. He had a life. Marlene didn't. "I stock shelves, bus dishes, do some grounds keeping."

"Does it pay well?"

Salena shot forward again. Her hands grasped the table edge. "I hope you're not asking him for money."

Romar knew she was asking just that. He'd expected she would ever since Salena mentioned it when she helped him write his letter. "It pays room and board, enough to cover the cost of this trip to meet you, hopefully enough to get me through another year of school. I've decided I don't want to be a high-school dropout."

Marlene glanced at Salena, then leaned closer to him. "It would help a lot if you could send me a little something. For incidentals."

He touched Salena's arm, a quick signal to let him handle it. "How much is a little something?"

"Twenty or twenty-five dollars a week. The state takes back half, so that doesn't leave me much."

He put his hands on the table, palms up. "Why do you need that much money? I mean, don't they provide you with everything?"

Marlene made a snorting sound. "State-issued hygiene products suck."

"Suck?" He leaned back, away from Marlene. "I don't even use that word, and I'm a teenage guy."

"Sorry, I mean they're harsh, like hard on your hair and skin. We have a store here where we can buy better products. Plus a treat now and then."

Salena hissed, "I can't believe you're asking this boy for money. Did you hear him say he's paying for room and board? And his own school expenses? Even his own medical insurance. And, it costs money to play sports. Of course, he could give all that up to take care of you."

"It's okay, Salena," he said. "Let me figure this out. Twenty or twenty-five dollars a week means you'd end up with forty or fifty dollars a month to spend at that store you mentioned. After they take out the half they keep."

"Not just at the store. I need to pay the office of support enforcement at least twenty-five dollars a month so they won't terminate my parental rights."

"Whoa, wait a minute. What parental rights?" That had been his latest worry, that she might have legal rights to him until he could be emancipated. Independent living was only a step toward legal adult status. Emancipation wouldn't happen until he turned sixteen.

"You have a sister. A half sister. Malena. She's eight, she's in foster care down in Vancouver. I had her with me until she turned five." Tears ran down Marlene's face. She wiped them with the back of her hand and sniffed. "Excuse me, I need to use the restroom."

A female officer materialized at their table.

"Everything okay here, Ms. Jones?"

"Uh huh. I'm just having a moment."

Marlene headed to the rest room. The officer moved on. Salena said, "Don't let her con you, Romie. You don't owe her."

"I'm on top of things," he said. "You need to let me handle this. If I handle it wrong, it's on me." He squeezed Salena's hand.

She squeezed back. "Here she comes. You're doing fine, Romar."

Marlene slid into her chair. "I'm sorry, it's hard sometimes, being in here and all."

"I can't send you money," Romar said. He wanted to say that having a half sister and not knowing about her made him feel sad. Mad, too, but sad more. He'd always wanted a brother or sister. "If Malena's in foster care, she's being seen to. I can't help you with the rest of it."

Marlene's pale brown eyes darkened. Her mouth hardened. She looked old and tired for a woman who would be thirty-two, maybe thirty-three.

"We're your only family," she said. "Think about that. You're denying your only family."

Her words carried venom that stung. He shook his head against the sting that hit him in the eyes. Having his own moment, he figured. "You're my birth mother, that's all. Dad and Granny were my family. Uncle Sherman and Aunt Joan are relatives. Aunt Arlene, too, though I don't know her. They're all legally family, but they don't feel like it. To me, they're my relatives. You're my relative. The people in Yachats who took me in and fed me and gave me a place to sleep are my family."

"You're hard, like your dad." Her words flew across the table, wet with saliva.

Romar resisted the urge to wipe away the dampness. He narrowed his eyes a bit to focus on her reaction when he answered. "I don't mind being like my dad. I wouldn't mind getting to know you, through letter writing. I'd like to meet my half sister someday."

"There's not much point, is there? You'll be twenty by the time I get out, the state will probably take Malena away from me, I'll be right where I've always been. Nowhere with nothing."

He stared at her, storing her pitiful look in his memory. At that moment he felt an overwhelming sorrow for his dad. He'd figured out back when his dad got the divorce papers that his mother had been pregnant when they got married. Now he saw the whole story. His dad got a girl pregnant and married her. The girl left him. His dad taught him responsibility by being responsible. He needed to write a letter to his dad, burn it and bury the ashes at his dad's grave site.

"That's up to you," he said. "Writing or not. If you do, I'll answer." He turned to Salena. "I think we better go. We've got a long drive home."

Kyra ran out of their motel room before Salena turned off the car engine. "What happened?" Why are you back so early? Was it awful?"

"Worse than awful," Salena said.

Romar was shaking his head. "No, it was okay. It answered all my questions."

Kyra grabbed his arm and pulled like it was a pump handle. "Tell me everything."

"He can tell you once we get checked out and on the road. Right now we need to call Vesta to catch her up."

Kyra dropped his arm and grabbed Salena's. "Are you mad, Salty? Or sad?"

"You better believe I'm mad. That woman wanted Romar to send her twenty-five dollars a week so she could buy junk food and pay child support for a sister Romar didn't know existed."

"A sister?" Kyra said. "You have a sister?"

"Half sister. Marlene said she's eight."

He told her everything he felt ready to tell by the time they reached the toll bridge that linked the Gig Harbor Peninsula with the city of Tacoma, a distance of eight miles. He opened his computer. "I'm going to write down some thoughts."

"We're going to stop for lunch, then drive straight through," Salena said. "We'll save those outlet stores for another day."

Romar wrote until the computer screen told him to back up his files, the battery was low.

22

HOME

Vesta came to the car with tears running down her face. "You're home." She wrapped her arms around him.

Romar hugged her back, bending to rest his chin on her shoulder so her tears could touch his face. "Home and free. That's how I feel. Like I'm the one that was in prison. Like not knowing what my mother looked like, not even from a picture, kept me . . . you know . . . from figuring out the last part of who I am."

"Oh, Romie, you're such a good young man. Come on, let's go inside and put on the closed sign."

"If that's true, that I'm good, it's because my dad kept me when I was born, and my granny helped him see to me. I learned a lot about choices while I was inside that prison, watching my mother and listening to her. She didn't want me. She left me so she could have her own life. She didn't want to be a mother, at least not then."

"Oh, Romie," she said again. She sounded so much like Granny that he had to grin.

"It's okay. I get it. She couldn't handle it. Maybe she was already using. Or drinking. Maybe we'd both be messed up if she'd tried to take care of me."

Vesta sniffed and dried her cheeks. Her eyes still glistened with tears.

"Hey," he said, "you got anything left to eat? Salty bought us lunch, and then we had a snack when we stopped for gas. After that, we had to fight over some old grapes in the cooler."

#

By mid-August Romar had been granted independent living status without enrolling in the state program that offered preparation through education, employment and life skills training. The social worker who came to see him said he didn't need that help.

She heard about his grades from Vesta, who wanted to post his transcript in the kitchen. He got her to put it on the desk in her office. She was getting to be so much like Granny that he saw both their faces when he looked at her.

"A three-point-five your freshman year," the social worker said. "Very impressive. You seem to be quite mature for your age, all things considered."

Romar made a noise that sounded like a horse snorting, apologized and said that most people didn't consider walking out of school two weeks before the year ended mature. His uncle and aunt certainly didn't.

"I have a report from them. Actually, I have several reports from Roseburg, from teachers, a counselor, and even a senior student, Josh Mobley. He gave you a ride, right? The day you left Roseburg?"

"Right."

"He said you two talked about basketball, that you were an outstanding player. He said he didn't know anything about your dad or grandmother, but that you must be in a world of hurt. His words. He said the Roseburg High basketball team needed you."

"Yeah, well, guys say stuff, it's no big deal." He lowered his head, scratched at a spill he'd missed when he wiped the table. He didn't want her to see that it felt like a big deal to have Mobley say that about him. *Pride goeth before the fall.* Damn, he needed to get Whitley's quotes out of his head.

"Your aunt and uncle, Sherman and Joan Jones, are still a bit upset, but they said they couldn't fault your behavior prior to your leaving. Your uncle does consider you old enough to make your own way in the world. Apparently he went to work in a mill when he was your age."

"Right, and he's still there. Top of the ladder now, or something like that."

The case worker nodded. "They talked rather a lot about family duty. I made a personal note in my official report that they seemed relieved to hear you were petitioning for Independent Living. I have a copy of the trusteeship they oversee for you. Another copy will be in your legal papers when you receive them from the state."

"Really? I get to see it?"

"You should have seen it long ago."

Before Romar had time to tell Kyra all that news, Ian brought him information about his half sister.

"Malena Lopez," Ian said, "lives with an uncle and aunt who are her birth father's brother and sister-in-law. They're relative foster-care parents like your uncle and aunt, except they do take the state support funds. Malena's father is in prison, serving a twenty-year sentence. He and your mother were involved in the same crime, though he's clearly the one authorities saw as most responsible."

"So, the eight years she got isn't that much, in comparison," Romar said.

"I'd say she's lucky. Probably lucky to be alive, given how much meth they were reported to be producing. Fortunately, Malena's uncle and aunt have an adequate income and provide her with a pleasant home. They love her and would like to legally adopt her. They're concerned Marlene will go back to using illegal substances when she's released."

"Yeah, I wonder about that, too."

"It seems Marlene hasn't taken advantage of the parenting program the prison offers. She did get her GED, so she's qualified to enroll in skill-building programs. There are organizations that volunteer inside. One helps with family issues. Maybe your visit will spur her into getting involved in that. There's still hope for her, if she chooses to help herself. "

Romar scrubbed a hand over his face. "I keep thinking about what we read in that article you found on the web. The one that said all addicts' first and most important relationship is with their drug of choice."

Ian nodded. "And, you said she repeated that she's addicted, that it's a sickness, a disease."

"It's sad," Romar said. "To waste your life like that, I mean. She wanted me to understand her addiction. I guess I do, sort of. And there's another thing. If she'd stayed to raise me, I might not have had my granny around."

That night Romar wrote the last of the story he started in Salena's car when they were heading home. He planned to give Nora Findlay a copy when she and Tom came to Vesta's for Labor Day weekend. He'd tried to get a poem out of it for Whitley, but that wasn't happening. He copied the whole thing, over 4,000 words, into an email and wrote a note.

Dear Mr. Whitley,

Here's the assignment to make up for dissing detention. You wanted an explanation. This about covers it. You said a good poem requires knowing which words to cross out of a longer story. I know there's a poem in here. Maybe you can find it for me. Thanks for being a good teacher.

Sincerely, Romar Jones

The last week in August Romar went to Waldport High School to register as a new student. He'd filled out all the paperwork required and waited in line for someone to go over the forms. It felt weird to write Ian Gallagher's address on the forms, and even more weird to write *Independent Living Program* where it asked for parent or guardian.

He shuffled his feet a few times, aware of his new shoes that fit and the clothes he'd purchased for himself when Salty took him along on a shopping trip to the outlet stores in Lincoln City. He'd even gotten a haircut, thinking he might meet the basketball coach. Or at least see the school gym.

He looked at the students behind him, another ten or so, spotted a guy with curly hair and blinked. "Carlos?" he said.

"Hey, Romar Jones, my man, you a newbie like me?"

"You've got it. You live here? In Waldport?"

"Moved here along about the time we first met

The registrar called Romar's name. Carlos said, "Hey, hang around, catch me up on what gives with you."

By the time Ian picked him up for the trip back to Vesta's, Romar had learned that Carlos had a dad in Mexico, sent back there by the U. S. as an illegal. Carlos and his mom moved to Waldport when school got out. It sounded like his mom was trying to get away from some guy.

"See you next week," Romar said. He'd met some other kids. It would make the first day of school easier.

The last Wednesday in August, one week before the first day of school and two days before Labor Day weekend, Romar and Kyra walked through Yachats holding hands. "It's official," she said. "We're an item. But it's just that. No kissing in the corridors in school. I'm not into that."

"We'll see," he said.

He was still grinning when he strolled into Vesta's at six, an hour later than he'd planned to be back.

"Finally," Vesta said. "Oh, you're not late, you have a visitor who's been waiting all afternoon." She waved her arm at the tables that should have been empty, cleaned off and set up for morning.

A man stood and walked toward him. He held a file folder in his left hand.

"Mr. Whitley?" Sweat erupted. His ears felt hot. It looked like Whitley wasn't accepting his final paper as a poetry assignment.

"Jones," Whitley said. "I'm returning your final paper." He had the scowl that always developed five minutes into class.

"Hey, I did the best I could, it's just that I'm not really into poetry."

"But this is your work? You wrote this story yourself?" He opened the folder. It held a printout of the story Romar titled "*Home.*"

"Yeah. Yes sir, I wrote it."

"And it's all true?"

Romar took in a breath and blew it out. "Do you think I'd make up stuff like that?"

Whitley's scowl disappeared. His face relaxed. His mouth even stretched a bit. "Well, I thought you had a pretty good imagination, but no, this rings true. It's an amazing personal essay."

"Really?" Romar blinked, pushed at his glasses, shook his hands to loosen up, get ready for the next play.

"Really. I'd like to enter it in a teen essay contest, but I need your permission. You might not want your name known . . . if the piece gets published. The information about your mother. Sadly, I didn't know about that, or about your dad's death. Your aunt and uncle in Roseburg might not be wild about their role in your life being aired, even though you basically forgave them. You said you understood why they wouldn't be thrilled with a new responsibility. You even seem to understand your mother's choices."

"Yeah, or something like that."

Vesta, who'd left them to talk, came back with Romar's transcript. "Does this mean you'll erase the minus sign you put behind Romie's A?"

"I'll change it to a plus sign if he agrees the story can be entered in the contest. And if he shows me around the rest of this place he calls home. Yachats, Smelt Sands Beach, Bob Creek, the Cummins Creek Wilderness."

"You into hiking?"

"I've written poems out in the wilderness."

"Okay," Romar said. "It's a deal." He turned, took a jump shot. "Jones scores."

Whitley grinned.

"Sorry, sir, it's just that I'm more into basketball than poetry."

"Poetry is just one form of writing," Whitley said, grin still in place. "Basketball and writing are not polar opposites. You can be good at both."

Acknowledgements

For listening, critiquing and support, thanks to members of the Gig Harbor Wednesday Night Writers Group: Colleen Slater, Kathleen O'Brien, Kathryn Arnold, Frank Slater and Garner Conn. Thanks to Lucinda Wingard, Anna Verratti and Jana Bourne for Monday afternoons. Thanks to Eve Begley Kiehm, Susan Schnell and Marla Klipper for reading, and to Gretchen Russell for editing.

#

Thanks to the San Francisco Partnership for Incarcerated Parents for the following:

Children of Incarcerated Parents: A Bill of Rights

1. I have the right to be kept safe and informed at the time of my parent's arrest.
2. I have the right to be heard when decisions are made about me.
3. I have the right to be considered when decisions are made about my parent.
4. I have the right to be well cared for in my parent's absence.
5. I have the right to speak with, see and touch my parent.
6. I have the right to support as I struggle with my parent's incarceration.
7. I have the right not to be judged, blamed or labeled because of my parent's incarceration.
8. I have the right to a lifelong relationship with my parent.

Romar Jones Takes A Hike
Reader's Guide

1. Discuss the factors that entered into Romar's decision to take a hike when there are only two weeks remaining in the school year.

2. What does Romar learn about himself during the five days between leaving Roseburg High School and stopping at Vesta's by the Sea?

3. Romar is 15 ½ in this story. Should he have been reported as a Runaway Teen or a Missing Person? What difference would reporting his disappearance from Roseburg have made to this stage of his life?

4. What role does Julie Matlock pay in Romar's life?

5. What is the significance of Romar starting a poem when he reaches the Pacific Ocean? Is it to get a decent grade, or is it something deeper?

6. Food aromas draw Romar to Vesta's by the Sea. Was it a lucky coincidence that the stop led to Granny's relatives? Could it be destiny?

7. What emotions does Romar experience when he realizes his granny is related to Leila Jarvi, and that means he and Kyra are cousins?

8. Vesta and her friend Ian Gallagher play important but different roles in Romar's journey. Describe the roles each plays. Are their roles gender based?

9. How does Romar feel about Kyra's plan to make him the lone male in the extended Jarvi family?

10. How does Romar's first hike into the national forest across from Vesta's by the Sea help him sort out some truths about his dad?

11. On his second hike into the same area, Romar hears his dad's voice warning him of danger. How would you explain the voice?

12. The summer solstice weekend marks a turning point in Romar's story. What role does the Matlock family play? Tom and Nora Findlay? Vesta's story about her former caretaker? The couple Romar calls Fourteen?

13. Why does Salena Jarvi, Kyra's grandmother, make the arrangements to transport Romar to the Washington prison to meet his mother.

14. At the Yachats Fourth of July celebration, Romar meets some of Kyra's friends and classmates who will be his future classmates, too. How do you think the events of the day will impact his future?

15. When Vesta's former caretaker appears in the dark of a stormy night, Romar deals with him. Explain how that changes his relationship with Vesta.

16. How does finally meeting his mother help Romar prepare to go on with his life?

17. This story begins with Romar walking out of Mr. Whitley's language arts class during a poetry discussion. How do you feel about how this story concludes?

18. Basketball and poetry are used as metaphors in this story. How are they similar? How do they differ in developing Romar's character?

CPSIA information can be obtained at www.ICGtesting.com
Printed in the USA
BVOW021914071011

273112BV00001B/22/P

9 780982 820599